ALSO BY A.P. FUCHS

BLOOD OF MY WORLD TRILOGY

DISCOVERY OF DEATH
MEMORIES OF DEATH
LIFE OF DEATH

UNDEAD WORLD TRILOGY

BLOOD OF THE DEAD
POSSESSION OF THE DEAD
REDEMPTION OF THE DEAD

THE AXIOM-MAN™ SAGA

(LISTED IN READING ORDER)

AXIOM-MAN or
AXIOM-MAN: TENTH YEAR ANNIVERSARY
SPECIAL EDITION
EPISODE NO. 0: FIRST NIGHT OUT
DOORWAY OF DARKNESS
EPISODE NO. 1: THE DEAD LAND
CITY OF RUIN
EPISODE NO. 2: UNDERGROUND CRUSADE
OUTLAW
EPISODE NO. 3: RUMBLINGS
OF MAGIC AND MEN (COMIC BOOK)

MECH APOCALYPSE

MECH APOCALYPSE

OTHER FICTION

A STRANGER DEAD
A RED DARK NIGHT
APRIL (WRITING AS PETER FOX)
MAGIC MAN (DELUXE CHAPBOOK)
THE WAY OF THE FOG (THE ARK OF LIGHT VOL. 1)
DEVIL'S PLAYGROUND (WITH KEITH GOUVEIA)
ON HELL'S WINGS (WITH KEITH GOUVEIA)

Zombie Fight Night: Battles of the Dead
Magic Man Plus 15 Tales of Terror
Undeniable
The Dance of Mervo and Father Clown
Flash Attack: Thrilling Stories of Terror, Adventure, and Intrigue

Anthologies (as editor)

Dead Science
Elements of the Fantastic
Vicious Verses and Reanimated Rhymes: Zany Zombie Poetry for the Undead Head
Metahumans vs the Undead
Bigfoot Terror Tales Vol. 1 (with Eric S. Brown)
Bigfoot Terror Tales Vol. 2 (with Eric S. Brown)
Metahumans vs Werewolves

Non-fiction

Book Marketing for the Financially-challenged Author
Canadian Scribbler: Collected Letters of an Underground Writer
Look, Up on the Screen! The Big Book of Superhero Movie Reviews
Getting Down and Digital: How to Self-publish Your Book
The Canister X Transmission: Year One
The Canister X Transmission: Year Two
The Canister X Transmission: Year Three

Poetry

The Hand I've Been Dealt
Haunted Melodies and Other Dark Poems
Still About A Girl

WWW.CANISTERX.COM

by

A.P. FUCHS

with Jeff Burton

Coscom Entertainment
WINNIPEG

The fiction in this book is just that: fiction. Names, characters, places and events either are products of the author's imagination or are used fictitiously. Any resemblance to actual events or persons living or dead, or any known superheroes and/or supervillains is purely coincidental.

ISBN 978-1-927339-70-1

Axiom-man and all other related characters are Trademark ™ and Copyright © 2018 by Adam P. Fuchs. All rights reserved.

Auroraman and all other related characters are Copyright © 2018 by Jeff Burton. All rights reserved.

AXIOM-MAN/AURORAMAN: FROZEN STORM is Copyright © 2018 by Adam P. Fuchs and Jeff Burton. All rights reserved, including the right to reproduce in whole or in part in any form or medium.

Published by COSCOM ENTERTAINMENT

Check out AXIOM-MAN on the web at www.canisterx.com

Text set in Garamond; Printed and Bound in the USA

COVER ART BY JUSTIN SHAUF AND DONOVAN YACIUK

A.P. Fuchs: This is for Axiom-man fans everywhere. Thank you for supporting the Kickstarter that made this novella possible. And if you're a new reader, thank you for joining Axiom-man and Auroraman on their icy adventure.

Jeff Burton: I would like to dedicate this first and foremost to my wife Melinda and our five amazing children. Without your love and support I couldn't do any of this. Also, some huge thanks has to go to Ted and Andrew. You two set this wheel in motion and I hope I am making it all you hoped it could be.

A TALE OF TWO HEROES

An Introduction
by
A.P. Fuchs

YOU KNOW, TO be perfectly honest with you, I can't remember how I found out about Auroraman. Most likely through Facebook, but let's not put that in stone. Then I found out either right then and there or shortly afterward that Axiom-man cover artist Justin Shauf was working on an Auroraman tale. Then, after that, I found out Auroraman had a Kickstarter for a comic book, and it was a successful Kickstarter at that, all helmed by Jeff Burton. Here was a guy who truly believed in his character, even dressed as his character, heck, even made the character his alter ego in four-color panels.

I was amazed and intrigued because I, too, had a superhero I believed in: Axiom-man. The first Axiom-man novel came out in 2006 and we're eight books into the series so far out of a planned fifty.

Suddenly, the light bulb went off. What if I approached Jeff and asked if we could do an Axiom-man/Auroraman Kickstarter? So I did, and it just so happened Jeff was already planning another one to fund another comic so I offered to write a novel that would team up the two characters. He thought it was a brilliant idea and agreed.

We launched the Kickstarter and, well, here we are almost a year later as I write up this introduction, one of the final pieces before the book you hold in your hands goes to press.

Writing *Frozen Storm*—of which you can find the prelude to in the pages of *Auroraman* No. 1—was fun, challenging, and gave me a chance to play in another character's world. See, Axiom-man and Auroraman don't come from the same universe, so the question was, how do we team these two together? The answer was in the *The Axiom-man Saga*. During one of the storylines (*Doorway of Darkness*), temporary portals were created and appeared every so often. My agenda with these was so Axiom-man could fight otherworldly super types or monsters, them coming from a portal a piece of their origin story. I told this to Jeff and he stunned me when he said that Auroraman's staff can detect portals and accidentally trigger them. So there you go: I had my in.

I also wanted our heroes to fight a near-impossible-to-beat bad guy, the idea being it took the two of them to take him down. The ice monster idea—I don't remember who said it first, me or Jeff—regardless, I liked it and decided to run with it. Every time I had a question or an idea for the book, I'd bounce it off Jeff and, thankfully, he always agreed it was a good idea and so I wrote that idea out during the next writing session.

One of the challenges I faced when crafting the tale was to give Axiom-man and Auroraman equal screen time. I didn't want to lean one way or the other so that fans of each character got an equal dose of that character instead of reading about someone else and just waiting for their superhero to show up.

What also marks this book as unique is that I gave Jeff a copy of the first draft. The *first*. Something I've never done to anyone in all the books I've written. I always give my editor my third draft. That was the draft I planned on giving Jeff, but he couldn't wait. Bottom line? He loved the story and was happy with it.

My hope as you read this tale of two heroes is you'll enjoy it as much as Jeff did and enjoy it as much as I enjoyed writing it. You're getting two superheroes for the price of one.

Now bundle up. It's getting cold. I hear a storm's coming.

A frozen storm.

- A.P. Fuchs
Winnipeg, MB

AXIOM-MAN / AURORAMAN
FROZEN STORM

Prologue

WHY IS IT so damn cold out? Frank thought. *I swear I've never lived in a colder city in all my life. Winnipeg—geez, get away from me and go bother someone else.*

Navigating the icy sidewalks took time. After pulling a George Thoroughgood at Dave's Bar—one bourbon, one scotch, and one beer . . . and then some—Frank had to heel-toe it across the ice lest he find himself twisting an ankle, or worse.

Wretched city. Wretched life, he thought. Newly separated, Frank Watson had lost everything—everything worth keeping, that was. Lost his kids. Lost his home. Lost his car. Lost everything to his ex. Sad part was, he had been the one who left, but he couldn't handle the way she'd treated him any longer. Now the kids had to grow up without a father and, who knew? Somewhere down the line another man would enter his ex-wife's life and take over the role that was supposed to be his. Frank winced at the pang sticking its sharp blade into his heart and tried swallowing down the guilt that twisted his stomach into a knot then turned it inside out and backward.

Maybe he should go back for the kids' sake? But, of course, if he did that, he'd be miserable. But was it worth it? One to suffer so three could be happy? Wasn't that what love was? Laying your life down for your family and sticking to them regardless of cost?

He didn't know. Maybe he wasn't capable of loving. He thought he'd been. He'd had a couple of girlfriends in the past prior to meeting his ex. He knew what love was and what he was capable of offering if with the right person. Besides, he was still in the separation stage of all this; the tail end of it, but still in it. It wasn't too late to go back. He didn't have to file for divorce. He could leave the option open.

Frank's head swooned at what had to be the scotch hitting him again. He paused on the sidewalk and tried to shake the double vision from his eyes with a few left-rights of his head.

Easy, Tiger, he thought, then whispered the same. "Now you're calling yourself 'Tiger.' Dumbass." The guy who walked past him gave Frank a double take. He must have heard him muttering to himself.

The snow started to come down in thick, giant flakes that would quickly pile up on everything and make it all look like a city made of marshmallows. The north wind didn't help either. With the wind chill, Frank suspected, it was at least minus forty-five. Probably more.

He turned a corner, lost in his own haze of booze. He shouldn't have drank so much. Too many bucks down the drain. Man, he had to pee. Somewhere in the distance were what he thought were cries for help along with some screams, but it could have been his imagination. Didn't matter. This was Winnipeg and crime was on the rise. People were turning up dead more and more frequently, the killer never caught, though most people, including Frank, knew who was responsible—Redsaw. That man clad in red and black with those haunting eyes had to be behind it. The superpowered villain had killed before. Plenty before. Frank swore if he ever came across the guy he'd give him the old one-two if able—before Redsaw would slaughter him, of course. Tough to go up against a guy who could shoot hot, red energy beams from his hands then take off into the sky like it was no big deal.

FROZEN STORM

Frank slipped on a patch of ice beneath the freshly-fallen snow, caught his balance, then kept going. He pulled a pack of cigarettes from his pocket, turned away from that piercing north wind to light up, then cautiously moved forward. It could have been his imagination, but the temperature seemed to have dropped. That or the warmth of the hard booze had left him.

Man, he really had to pee.

Frank shook the snow off his brown leather jacket. *Should have worn gloves,* he thought.

His blond moustache and beard froze to his face in thick, white crystals.

A beard's supposed to keep you warm in the winter, he thought, *not freeze you to death!*

After a few cusses, he thought about how badly he had to pee again.

Frank turned into the nearest alley, hoping to find a spot so he could relieve himself. He found a garbage can. *Good enough.*

After finishing up and a sudden chill running through him, Frank looked down the alley.

"What the—" About thirty feet away was this vertical floating black mist—and a sudden flash of light blue disappearing into it. Frank would know that blue anywhere.

Axiom-man.

Lucky bugger. Doesn't have a care in the world, I bet, he thought. *If I had superpowers, I'd have nothing to worry about either. Would make life so easy. Heck, I could even be a hero.* He stumbled back a few steps, taking a few more drags off his cigarette as he slowly approached the line of black mist. It was maybe only a foot or two wide, around five or six feet tall, and hovered just above the ground.

"What is that thing?" he said.

He got closer, and by the time he finished his cigarette, he stood right next to it. Heart picking up pace a little, he wondered if—*Should I? No, you idiot. You don't know what it is. Yet . . .*

He reached out a near frost-bitten hand, his trembling fingers just grazing the black mist. They passed through it like steam off a kettle . . . but it was warm. Frank ran his hand through it again, the warmth it emitted sending oh-so-good comforting goosebumps throughout his body. He reached out his other hand and with his fingers started tickling the edges, each touch warming him.

"Oh, this feels amazing," he whispered. He'd always been fond of the goosebumps that came after being cold then suddenly being blasted with a wave of heat. Like putting on clothes fresh from the dryer.

He tickled the strange black mist's sides again . . . and it was then the black mist reached out and coiled a part of itself around his forearm and yanked his snow-covered body straight into the dark.

Frank spun around to try and see where the opening to this warm place was and couldn't see a thing. Sheer darkness. Freaking out, he ran to where he thought the opening might be but found none. The ice cold of melting snow running off his hair and in between his collar and skin and down his back sent a violent chill up his spine. Suddenly shivering, he brushed the snow off his jacket, but no matter how much he tried, every ounce of snow he brushed off suddenly resurfaced beneath his touch. Frantic, he shook himself like a dog, stomped his feet, brushed his clothes, ran his fingers through his frosty beard.

The snow and ice wouldn't come off.

Would. Not. Come. Off.

FROZEN STORM

Screaming, cold snow climbed off his beard and covered his cheeks while other cold tendrils of ice went inside his mouth and down his throat. He clamped his mouth shut, but it was too late. The ice was inside of him. His ribs locked up in frozen pressure and then an explosion of cold radiated from his chest and through his limbs, freezing his bones. Snow ran off his jacket and covered his hands. He shook them, yelling and screaming, trying to get the snow off.

But it wouldn't come off . . . and screaming only made it worse as more ice and snow got into his mouth, giving him a brain freeze that forced him to his knees and press his hands against his head.

Rocking back and forth and shrieking from the pain, Frank squeezed his eyes shut as the ice touched his eyeballs. Every muscle—one by one—spasmed and locked.

Though conscious and aware, he couldn't move. Just a block of what he presumed was ice in a dark hole.

Minutes passed. Hours. Seconds. He didn't know. There was no time in this place, only some perception of things happening but not always linearly.

Ice exploded up Frank's throat, and he opened his mouth to throw up frosty bits of whatever was inside his stomach.

Then warmth . . . as if this black mist rushed to his rescue. It went into his mouth, down his throat, and filled his entire being, thawing his muscles and bones. Then the warmth stopped, and he was neither hot nor cold.

Bringing his hands together, Frank gasped when it felt like he had just brought two thick pieces of glass against each other. He clapped and the glass shattered. He tried feeling his hands again only to find them covered in glass. Using the only item of touch he could, he brought the back of his hand to his mouth and licked it. His hand was cold.

Ice.

He ran his fingers all over himself, met with the same thing. Just a layer of ice covering him. He slammed his hands together. Slammed his forearms together. Bashed his knees with his palms. Anything to get the ice off.

But it remained.

A light shone, there, just up ahead.

Whispers. A language he didn't understand. Each word and syllable penetrating his skull and going right into his brain. *Tilmir. Phornifer. Grolinait.* Anger burst forth in his heart and seemed to invigorate him.

The world hated him, he knew. Even this place of darkness despised him.

A rush of wind pushed him from behind and sent him toward the slit of light ahead. Its opening was even thinner than the one he had entered when first coming into this place of blackness. The closer he got, the more he saw—green grass and a blue sky.

Up to the opening, furious at what happened, furious at his life, furious at himself—Frank reached out his ice crystal hand and touched light on the other side of the veil.

Chapter One

"Who are you?" Axiom-man asked the man floating before him. Then, "Who—"

He looked down at the portal he'd emerged from. The thing balled together into a black cloud and vaporized. "No!" Axiom-man said and flew down to where the portal once was. Grimacing, he flew straight up to the man with the long beard. "Did you do this? Did you pull me through? Do you have any idea of what you've done?"

"Easy there, friend, I just" —the man with the long beard holding a wooden staff with a glowing green ball on the end of it pointed it at him— "You're flying."

"So are you. Who are you? Where am I?

"My name's Aurora—"

Axiom-man ignored him and once more flew down to where the portal used to be. If this guy floating above him had indeed triggered it, if he had indeed bridged the gap between two worlds—he just created one hell of a problem. Axiom-man had been through this before when he entered what he dubbed "The Dead Land," a post-apocalyptic world full of zombies, a place where he encountered a dark version of himself. Finding a way home had been nearly impossible, and now—his heart sank. These portals just didn't open up any old time. They were residual clouds from when the Doorway of Darkness had been opened and the black clouds from within it spilled out. Axiom-man thought that, perhaps, the portals only led to dark places, but right now all didn't seem so bad. The grass was green. The sky blue with bright white clouds.

And a flying man in a leather jacket, holding a big staff above him.

Axiom-man flew up to him. "Look, I'm sorry, but I need you to do what you just did. Open another door. Please, um—"

It took a moment for the other man to pick up the cue. "Auroraman." He held out a big hand for a handshake.

Readying his eye beams in case this was some sort of trap, Axiom-man shook it, and when nothing happened other than a plain old handshake, he let go but still kept blue energy coated over his eyes in case this guy tried something. There was no way he could trust him. Everybody that he had met who had superpowers was never a good seed and always caused destruction: Redsaw, Bleaken, Battle Bruiser, Lady Fire.

"I—" Auroraman started. "Nice to meet you and" — he stroked that long brown beard of his— "nice costume?" He said it like a question.

I can't tell him it's nice to meet him, too. I don't know him. "Same, I suppose. Looks like you went with the more casual look?"

The two men hovered in the air, awkward.

"I need you to open the portal again," Axiom-man said, "if indeed that's what you did."

"I did. This staff" —Auroraman hefted its weight— "has great power and finding doors between worlds is one of them. As much as I'd like to talk, clearly you're in a hurry, so I'll see what I can do." The ball at the end of the staffed crackled with green lightning and Auroraman flew down to where the portal had been. He rotated the staff in his hand, moved a few feet one way, did the same, moved a few feet the other way, did the same.

Axiom-man flew down to meet him.

FROZEN STORM

"It's not working," Auroraman said. "The portal's gone."

"Look, whatever I caused, I'm sorry," Auroraman said.

"What you caused . . . was leaving my world without someone to stop a madman," Axiom-man said.

"I'm so sorry. I—"

"I'm not going to say it's okay. I can't. But let's try and find another portal. Clearly that staff of yours did something. Use it. However that is, use it."

Auroraman nodded. "It can detect bridges between worlds when the globe is near them."

"How near?"

"Difficult to say. It's almost spontaneous. Could be a few feet. Could be a hundred feet. Depends on the pull of the globe and on the strength of the portal."

"Does this globe have a memory bank?"

Auroraman eyed the green glowing globe. "In a sense. It grows accustomed to its user and what transpires around it. Frankly, this staff is a relatively new discovery. I'm still learning how it works." Auroraman focused and tried to bend the staff to his will.

Search, he thought. *Find the black cloud. Remember Axiom-man. Remember the blue. Remember what you did.*

The globe glowed a slightly brighter green, then returned to its normal color: green light in a sphere of swirling fog and haze.

"We need a Plan B," Axiom-man said.

"Perhaps the portal is still around, just unseen by our eyes."

"Could be. I can feel them, in a way," Axiom-man said. "They're—never mind. It's a long story."

Auroraman led the way as the two flew through the air and over the forest below, his eyes fixed on the globe the entire time. Axiom-man seemed to also have his mind elsewhere.

Probably seeing if he could sense something as well, Auroraman thought.

The two finished their sweep above the tree line then descended into the forest itself, zig-zagging in between the trees. Sometimes they remained high by the forest's canopy; other times low to the ground; and yet other times somewhere in between.

An hour passed.

Then two.

Then three.

They emerged from the forest. "We've covered every square inch," Axiom-man said.

"We did. It could be anywhere." Auroraman looked to the green prairie beyond and the wheat field just beyond that. "Follow me."

Axiom-man did and the two sped over the prairie, exchanging heights and sometimes flying next to one another. They even went over the wheat field: back and forth, back and forth, moving over a little each time.

They stopped mid-air, hovering.

"It's gone," Axiom-man said softly. Then screamed, "It's gone!" He tore off into the sky, leaving Auroraman alone.

Okay, stay calm, just breathe, Axiom-man thought then whispered the same. "Breathe." *You can get back. Just ask him to search far and wide. Find out some info. Get it done so you can go home.*

He wondered if the passage of time here was parallel to the passage of time in his own world. He admitted, though, that the warm sun felt good through his costume. It beat the frozen cold of the city he'd just come from.

Don't dwell on the niceties, he thought. *Do your job.*

He flew back down and met Auroraman. "I'm sorry. I know I'm on edge. Things are real bad back home. Bodies . . . so many bodies showing up in cities across the country. Only one man can be responsible for so many: Redsaw."

"Redsaw?"

"He's like me. Stronger, in fact. More powerful. He's tearing Canada—my Canada—apart. I need to get back."

"I will help you, my friend. I got you into this. I will get you out."

"Oh yeah? How? We couldn't find the portal with that stick of yours."

"And you couldn't find it with that 'sensing' of yours."

Fair enough. "Then let's work together so I can go home."

Chapter Two

Frank watched the two men in the sky. The one in the long blue cape he knew—Axiom-man—but this other fellow, the man in the leather jacket with a long beard and strange staff, he didn't.

He looked at his hands. His fingers glistened in the sun . . . and did not melt. A whirlwind of an ice-cold tornado spun deep within. It seemed to radiate outward, filling his limbs with rock-solid—ice-solid—strength. Even his vision—something was different about it. Dancing through the air were thin stripes of blue. One floated past him. He reached out to touch it, and his frozen hand absorbed it. Could he see the cold currents in the air? If so, his ability to seemingly absorb them might come in handy—an endless supply of power.

Those men up there, far away, talking and seeming to be at peace with each other. Their talking gave away one thing: on some level they were allies. If they were friends or if Axiom-man even had any, he didn't know. But there were two of them up there and only one of him.

Frank.

Alone and covered in ice. He smashed his fist against a tree and instead of breaking his hand, wood chips blew out from beneath the bark.

Power, he thought. *Finally. Something actually going for me.*

He needed to explore this power. Needed to find out what he could do.

Frank retreated into the forest and remained unseen like he had before when the two flying men seemed to be searching for something. Then it dawned on him: they'd been looking for a way home. At least, Axiom-man had to be and had enlisted the other guy's help.

Frank didn't want to go home. Didn't want to return to the pain of losing his family. Here, in this new world, he could make a home of his own.

And he would be king.

———

"So, you don't know who I am?" Axiom-man asked, feeling extraordinarily vain about the question.

"No," Auroraman said. "Should I? Are you one of those 'shadow vigilantes'?"

"No. I was just making sure there wasn't another version of me in your universe. I've been down that road when I found myself in a zombie-infested city that ran parallel to my own. I didn't like what I found." *Unless indeed there is a version of me here that operates from the shadows. Thanks for getting inside my head, Auroraman.*

"What about me? Is there a me in your world?"

"No. Just a few others that can do things other people can't."

There was silence for a moment as they soared through the air. Auroraman still had his eyes on his staff, which meant he hadn't given up on searching for a portal. "I suppose that's a good thing, having a limit on enhanced humans. If what they are in your world are indeed human."

"They are, so far as I know. I hope the same is true for you."

The two flew over a small city. "Home," Auroraman said. "Humboldt, Saskatchewan."

I'm in Saskachatoon? Axiom-man thought, using the Winnipegger's slang for the province.

From what he can see this high up, it appeared to be a nice quiet place to live.

"I like it here," Auroraman said, seemingly to himself than to Axiom-man.

"Seems easier to contain. Less square mileage."

"And you're from?"

"Winnipeg."

"A big small town."

"They call it that here, too?"

"Yep." Auroraman came to an abrupt stop mid-flight. "I'm sorry, but the staff is picking up nothing."

Axiom-man's heart ached. He needed to get back home. "Let's hope it finds something so I'm not trapped here indefinitely."

"Are you your city's only hope?"

"Against Redsaw, yes. Against other powers, no."

"What powers do you have? Besides flight, of course."

Axiom-man thought about it for a moment. This could all be one big set up, with Auroraman feigning being nice. The man in the leather jacket could have indeed brought him here on purpose. Could even be an agent of Redsaw's if Redsaw had connections between worlds. There was no way to know. "I'd rather not share, if it's all the same."

Auroraman looked disappointed, but nodded. "Fair enough. I wouldn't disclose my abilities to a complete stranger either. But," he said, "let me assure you, I am one of the good guys."

Time will only tell on that one, Axiom-man thought.

The screeching and roar of wheels below drew both men's attentions.

Something bad was going down.

Chapter Three

Frank looked at his hands, and without effort or thought, an icy mist rose from them. It swirled and dusted the air.

The sun.

Despite being out in what he assumed was twenty-five Celsius weather, he wasn't melting nor even hot.

Frank concentrated on his hands.

Grow. Bigger, he thought. The mist responded immediately and coalesced into snow, which then rose then fell back into his hands. He imagined the snow again, and once more snowflakes blossomed from his hands and rose into the air and, like before, drifted down into his hands.

"I'm . . . I'm . . ." He didn't know what he was, but there was power here. Frozen power. Cold power. With a grimace, he imagined the ice and snow starting at his shoulders, deep within his bones, then surging through his bones and muscles and bursting forth from his hands. Cold swept through his arms and a blast of ice shot forth, freezing the tree in front of him an icy gray. The leaves were crystals, the bark gray and glimmering with specks of ice.

Smiling, Frank reached up and channeled icy power through his arms, this time imagining it coming from his core. Giant spikes of ice grew forth from his hands and rose higher and higher until they toppled after some forty feet. They crashed through the trees, breaking branches as they fell, their ice not crumbling.

Frank turned and imagined a little dart of ice shoot from his hand. The sliver of cold formed and hit the frozen tree like an arrow sinking into its target.

After a deep breath, which stung like fresh mint, Frank exhaled an icy fog. It crystalized on the air, and he broke through its mist, hearing it crackle around him as it crashed against his ice-covered body.

He once more gazed at his hands, his torso, his legs, his feet.

Pure ice.

Solid as steel.

Invincible.

The Brinks truck whipped around the corner. The back was open, and men with machine guns fired at the cops chasing them.

"A regular occurrence in your city?" Axiom-man asked.

"Not really," Auroraman said, "but I have noticed an increase in crime ever since I became, well, me."

"Same thing in my world. Redsaw showed up not long after I did. We're tied together, him and I, but that's a story for another time, if we ever get around to it."

Below, tires popped as bullets pierced the rubber. The cop car swerved and plowed into a storefront.

"I'll grab the truck, you check the store," Auroraman said.

"Fair enough." Axiom-man changed course and headed toward the cop car.

Auroraman gripped his staff, straightened his sunglasses, and flew hard toward the Brinks truck. In an instant, the bullets started flying like horizontal rain.

FROZEN STORM

Auroraman flew up above the stream of gunfire only for the men to adjust their shot to try and take him down.

Can't let them get away, he thought. His staff lit up before him as a barrage of bullets ripped through the air. They bounced off the staff-generated force field. Auroraman flew lower, powered down, and got himself back in line with the truck. It was a fool's errand because just as he was about to blast one of the tires out from under the truck, another wave of bullets flew his way. Once again, he initiated the force field. Despite the force field being nearly invincible, he still felt the bullets' force, like rain striking an umbrella.

"This has got to stop," he muttered. *Who knows how many bullets ricocheted off the force field and hit others? Hopefully none.*

With a shout, Auroraman flew faster toward the truck. He blocked bullets again, then came up alongside the rear end of the truck and sent a blast of green energy into one of the metal doors. The door slammed shut, wedging itself in its frame. Quickly, he flew up and over to the other side and did the same to the other door, locking the men in.

Now, the driver.

A shotgun blast narrowly missed Auroraman as he approached the front of the truck. Sirens whirred in the distance then quickly got louder. Assistance was on its way but not before—Auroraman set up his shield once more as boom after boom rocked the air. This time, each bounce of the bullet against his shield was like staving off a barrage of punches through a sheet of wood and hoping it didn't break.

The moment the gunfire stopped, he was finally able to fire a blast into the front tires, causing the vehicle to skid. He flew out of its way, then, from behind, used a beam of green light from his staff to slide the vehicle to safety. Cop cars whipped by beneath him. The second the Brinks truck was motionless, the driver opened an unharmed door and ran.

Cops fired at him.

A bullet struck the guy and he fell.

Auroraman flew over the police and landed beside the man. As he crouched down, he once again used the force field to protect the man from any more gunfire.

"You okay?" he asked the driver.

"I'm shot in my damn leg, so no, I'm not okay!"

The cops were already on foot, walking toward the two of them, guns drawn.

"You gotta help me, man," the driver said. "They're gonna take me in and I ain't goin' to no prison. Know what they do to guys like me in there?"

It took a moment for Auroraman to figure out what the guy meant, but once he did, he shook his head. The guy was a rapist. Prison would eat him alive.

"I'm sorry," Auroraman said. "I can't help you." He turned to the cops, deactivated the force field, then held out his hand to stop them. "It's okay. He's down. Please put your weapons away."

Some obeyed, some didn't. With a heavy heart, Auroraman took to the sky. The cops could take it from here. Even eventually pry the remainder of the crew from the Brinks truck.

Somewhere out there was a man in a blue cape. Someone Humboldt hadn't seen before.

Axiom-man had finished helping the cops from their vehicle by the time Auroraman landed beside him.

FROZEN STORM

Auroraman must've noticed the door ripped from its hinges because he met Axiom-man with a grin.

"All is well?" Auroraman asked.

"You tell me. Did you get them?"

"Got them."

"Good." Axiom-man stepped away from the cops. They were about to ask questions and he didn't have time to explain anything to them. Ideally, he'd like to keep as low a profile as possible in this other world. Priority one was getting home. He looked up and took to the sky. Auroraman was soon beside him.

"How many were there?" Axiom-man asked.

"Five."

It seemed Auroraman expected a reply by the way he tipped his glasses down at him, but Axiom-man didn't give one. As long as the men were captured, that was all that mattered. He wasn't looking for a partner or even a friend right now. An ally, fine, but that would be as far as it could—or would—go. He already knew not to mess with other worlds from that undead one he visited.

No matter what happened, he'd keep a low profile.

No matter what.

Chapter Four

"I swear I saw something," Mike said as he and Angela navigated their way through the forest's trail.

"Me, too. Like . . . trees . . . no, wait, pillars. Crystal."

"Ice?"

"How? It's summer, dingbat." She gave him a playful swat.

"You're right. But still . . . crystals? Really? How is that even possible? Maybe we saw the sunlight glimmering through the leaves or something, and at just the right angle and—"

"Now you're changing your mind?" she said.

"Well . . ."

"Come on. Let's keep going. Whatever made those things has to be around here somewhere."

Angela walked on, but Mike stopped in his tracks. "Really think that's a good idea?"

"Beats standing around here arguing about it."

"True." He jogged up to her. "Let's see what we'll see."

It wasn't long before the air took on a chill. Mike rubbed his bare arms.

Angela did the same. "Brrr . . ."

"I know it's 'brrr,'" he said.

"Will you leave me alone?" Her tone took on a snap, and Mike knew to leave her be.

A little bit further and Mike saw his breath. Angela's came out in thick puffs. Yet a little further still and the surrounding trees became frost covered. Mike stepped up to one of them and ran his finger along the bark. It was ice-cold.

FROZEN STORM

"Crazy," he said quietly.

"No kidding. Dare you to stick your tongue to it?"

"Ha. Ha." He placed his whole palm on the tree. It was so cold his skin stuck a little when he pulled it away. "Angela" —he put his palm against it again— "you should feel this." He didn't hear her move toward him. "Angela?" The bark was so cold it chilled him to the bone and his hand began to ache. "Angela?"

Nothing.

Mike spun around. "Angela?"

She was frozen solid, like a mannequin of ice. And it was her. It was definitely her. He knew those ringlets in her hair. Knew those squinty eyes and that nose that was slightly too big for her face.

"Angela?" Fear seizing him, the cold digging under his skin, Mike shouted, "Help! Someone! Help!"

"Shh," someone said. "They'll hear you."

He turned toward the voice.

A man made of ice came toward him.

"Okay, let's get back on task here and find me a way home," Axiom-man said as he and Auroraman flew through the clouds.

"Agreed. As much fun as that was, you don't belong here."

"Fun? You call that fun? Crime is fun?"

"That's not what I meant. What I meant was we did a good job."

"Then you should have said that."

Auroraman didn't like Axiom-man's tone, but he couldn't blame the guy for being snippy. If he found himself off-world, he'd probably be on edge, too.

"Just do what you can with that staff of yours. Find a portal. A black cloud. Something," Axiom-man said.

"Working on it." *Working on it.*

Frank sat in the darkness, alone. It was pitch black in every direction. The smell—there was none. Just—air. There was something pure about this place, something deep, something serene.

Whispers.

A language he didn't understand.

Words.

Tilmir. Phornifer. Grolinait.

Over and over again.

With each pass of the words, his heart burned hotter and hotter with rage, a solid yet continuously-moving anger that ran through his body head to toe.

Tilmir. Phornifer. Grolinait.

The power he'd been given. The gift. The ice.

Cold, hard power.

He couldn't help but dwell on it.

The rage went inferno . . . and his heart burst with terror yet with a comforting sense of dominance.

Tilmir. Phornifer. Grolinait.
Tilmir. Phornifer. Grolinait.

Frank remained in the darkness.

Tilmir. Phornifer. Grolinait.
Tilmir! Phornifer! Grolinait!

Yes, Frank thought. "Yes."

Tilmir! Phornifer! Grolinait!

TILMIR! PHORNIFER! GROLINAIT!

Frank opened his eyes.

FROZEN STORM

The two frozen people stood before him. So beautiful. So complete. So at rest.

Time passed . . . and one of them moved. Boy and girl. Man and woman.

Parents.

Like he used to be.

Tilmir. Phornifer. Grolinait.

He studied him. The man held all his features, just carved from ice. Same with the woman. He eyed them carefully. The man and woman began to move. They studied their hands and feet as if seeing them for the first time. Then they stopped and looked at Frank with subtle admiration and a gaze of askance in their eyes.

Frank thought, *Closer.* The two moved closer. *No way! Closer.* They moved again. Frank smiled. *Closer.* They were nearly right up to him. Frank raised his hand, and they mirrored him. He raised the other one, and they did the same.

Tilmir. Phornifer. Grolinait.

The words within. The whispers. It came from the darkness. It came from . . . the black cloud. The portal.

Frank let loose and sliced through a frozen tree with a beam of ice from his hand. The man and woman did likewise to the trees next to them.

"They're at my command," he whispered.

Tilmir. Phornifer. Grolinait.

"Come," he told them. "We have work to do."

Chapter Five

It was fruitless and hopeless.

Axiom-man hovered mid-air. He wasn't going home. Auroraman's staff picked up absolutely zero portals, never mind the specific one they were looking for. It was already getting late in the day. The only options were to fly around and look for something to do or keep searching for the portal.

"What's the crime rate in Humboldt?" Axiom-man asked. "Gotta be something fierce. What went down earlier was a pretty big deal."

"It's not bad. Regular stuff: burglaries, hold-ups, drunk drivers. Now and then something fantastic happens, but not often."

"Fantastic?"

"Superpowered."

"Ah, I see." Axiom-man thought about asking questions, but it was better left unsaid. This was Auroraman's town, and it'd be a dumb idea to compare rogue galleries.

"So, I ask again," Auroraman said, "what are your powers?"

Axiom-man was about to speak then thought better of it. "A suspicious one, aren't you? Look, I don't know you so I'd rather not say, if it's all the same."

"You don't trust anyone, do you?"

"These days, no. I've learned typically no good comes out of those with special abilities."

"I'd rather see the good in people than label them."

"I'm not labeling. Just playing it safe. No offense."

"None taken."

FROZEN STORM

They flew on, then went low, flying rooftop-level, keeping an eye out for anything that might demand their attention.

Thilmir. Phornifer. Grolinait.
Thilmir. Phornifer. Grolinait.

Frank was back in the dark, this time surrounded by swirls of black cloud. He knew this cloud. It was the portal. It was what brought him here. It was what somehow combined him and the snow.

It was what gave him his power.

Thilmir. Phornifer. Grolinait.

The whispers persisted, piercing like daggers, embedding themselves in his mind, his soul, his heart.

Those words—Comforting, like a fatherly friend. Dark, like something he knew was off limits and wasn't supposed to touch, but oh so appealing.

The clouds swirled about him, running through his body over and over. Snow fell, and he caught a glimpse of each flake before they were swallowed whole by the clouds.

Frank opened his eyes.

Thilmir. Phornifer. Grolinait.

He stepped forward and looked at his frozen zombies.

It was time.

"Shoot," Auroraman said. "I have a boy scout meeting. We're going over fire safety. Not sure if I should miss it or not."

"You do that stuff?"

Auroraman looked at him, his brow furrowed with a cross glare.

"That's not what I meant. I meant community service."

"Yes. Don't you?"

"I don't have time."

How can anyone not have time for their community? Auroraman thought. "Sorry to hear that."

"Go to your meeting. I'll hang around up here. Will keep an eye out, but will also try to stay as invisible as possible."

"Sounds like a plan to me. Catch you up here in a couple hours."

"Okay."

Auroraman dove down through the air and headed off to the scout meeting. The boys needed him. He was more than just their teacher: he was a mentor and father, especially to some. These kids needed strong role models to look up to. Some came from some pretty rough backgrounds.

Heroes do everything, big and small, he thought as he sailed through the air.

Axiom-man leaned back and folded his hands behind his head and floated along the air, using the thick white clouds beneath him as cover, centering himself. It'd been a long haul thus far, and the anxiety was already kicking in about what was going on back home. The crime. So many deaths. Redsaw.

"Two hours," he said to himself. "We need to track down a portal. I can't stay here. No way." He sighed, flipped over and stretched out his arms before him. The plan was to speed over the town and check for anything out of the ordinary. He'd only interfere if required. "My being here will raise too many questions. This needs to be a drop-in-get-out thing."

He lowered himself and flew below the cloud. As he headed toward town, he glanced back over his shoulder and caught a glimmer of something twinkling in the distance.

"Yes, rise," Frank said as he stood on an expanse of ice and grew ice walls past the forest's canopy. "Rise for me—Frank." The walls grew, and he inserted them wherever he could. He shot forth more ice, building up a ceiling. "Rise. Rise for Frank." He paused in his work. "No. Rise for" —*Thilmir. Phornifer. Grolinait*— "Crystallion."

Flecks of snow blew against Axiom-man's face the closer he got to that glimmer in the distance. As the thing came into view, he recognized the general area was where he had come through the portal.

"Oh no," he said. "What have I done now?"

The giant cube of ice with an incomplete roof stood before him. He flew down into it and found a few other walls within and a couple more ceilings.

He landed. *This is no good,* he thought. *Something came through the black cloud. Something cold.* "Way to go stating the obvious."

All around him were walls of ice about a foot thick. He pressed against one and retracted his hand a few moments after contact. The cold was so icy it pierced his skin even through his gloves and aura. A chill ran through him and he saw his breath.

"I need Auroraman right now," he said and tore into the sky.

Crystallion came out from behind one of the walls.

"That was close, wasn't it?" he said to his two frozen zombie disciples.

They didn't reply.

He got back to work building a structure worthy of someone of his stature. Axiom-man better not return, and especially not with that bearded fellow, but if they did, he'd be ready for them.

But not yet.

Soon.

First, there was something he needed to do.

"And that, kids, is how you build a campfire," Auroraman said.

The youngsters smiled. Suddenly, their attention looked upward. Many said, "Whoa."

Axiom-man floated down and landed beside Auroraman. "We need to go. Now."

Auroraman looked at the boy scouts. "I'm sorry, kids, but I have to go. Something's come up."

"Aww," said one.

"Who's the blue guy?" said another.

FROZEN STORM

"What's going on?" said one more.

"Trust me, boys," Auroraman said, "everything's all right." To Axiom-man, "Let's go."

The two hit the sky, leaving the boys behind.

Chapter Six

Crystallion stood with his two ice people before the town of Humboldt. His touch transformed those two hikers. Most likely, their touch would transform others.

"Whatever your names were before," Crystallion said, "are no more. You two were the first, my Adam and Eve. Those are your names now."

They nodded.

With Axiom-man and that other guy here, they were a threat to his power. Should he ever go to war with them, he wasn't sure if the victory would be his. He needed to know his strength would remain and that those two sky-dwellers wouldn't put an end to him.

Crystallion pointed toward Humboldt. "Go ye therefore and make me disciples of all peoples."

The two held out their hands and blasted ice from their fingertips, creating an icy path before them. Soon, they slid toward the town, the ice beneath their feet at their command.

―――

The structure had completely changed by the time Axiom-man and Auroraman returned to the ice fortress in the forest. It was no longer a simple cube with a few walls within, but rather an elaborate castle.

The frozen drawbridge was down.

Auroraman got his staff ready. He noticed Axiom-man's eyes crackle with blue energy. *Another one of his powers*, he thought.

"Carefully," Axiom-man said.

FROZEN STORM

"You don't have to tell me twice."

The two slowly entered and stood in the main foyer. A large, frozen winding staircase was before them that broke off into two wings. A hallway stretched off the floor they stood upon. Somewhere in here was whomever or whatever caused this.

"A person, most likely," Auroraman said.

"Huh?"

"The structure. Only something human—or humanoid—would've made it. Why else make a castle?"

"Yeah, but who or what are we dealing with?"

"Could be good, could be bad," Auroraman said.

"Probably bad," Axiom-man said. "So says my experience."

Auroraman gruffed, and the two stepped in further.

"Shall we?" Auroraman said.

Axiom-man nodded.

The two flew up the center staircase and split off, Auroraman heading right. Immediately, he found himself in a hallway with what looked like rooms off to each side. He slowed as he approached the first, then cautiously peered within, staff ready. The room was empty. Merely ice walls and nothing more.

He proceeded to the next one. Same thing. And the next. And the next, all rooms of ice, but that was all. Auroraman kept on, the hallway winding left in another loop. Plain or not, the ice work was astonishing. Aliens? There was no way to know. At least, not yet. Soon, he found himself face-to-face with Axiom-man.

"Find anything?" Auroraman asked.

"Nothing. Just empty rooms made of ice."

"Same here."

"We should check the lower level."

"Agreed."

The two stuck together and rounded the hallway back to the main staircase. Once on the main floor, they split off again.

Elsewhere, the ice burst forth from Crystallion's hands as he constructed the wall outside of town. That was step one.

Containment.

He slid along his ice trail, arms outstretched, sending forth blasts of ice in ten-or-so-foot sections, quickly building it layer by layer until each portion of the wall stood thirty feet high. It was going to take a while to hold in the city, and he was sure to build far enough away from it that no one would notice until it was too late.

Step two, well, that belonged to Adam and Eve.

Adam stepped onto Main Street and immediately those outside took note of his presence with gasps and shrieks. Somewhere off in the distance someone cried, "Auroraman!" It didn't faze him.

Go ye therefore . . . . The words echoed in Adam's mind. He headed toward the sidewalk where an elderly gentleman walked, leaning on a cane. The old timer must've been deaf—perhaps even partly blind—because he didn't move when Adam stepped up to him.

Adam put a hand on his shoulder and ice spread out from his touch, encasing the man. The old fellow must have felt a chill because suddenly that cane of his was in motion and he swung it at Adam. The wood snapped in two when it struck Adam's rock-hard ice body.

FROZEN STORM

Ice travelled over the man and encased him.

People shrieked.

Very clearly: "Auroraman, help!"

Someone to the right, coming closer: "Hey, buddy, you can't just . . ." The words caught in the man's throat.

Adam picked him up by the neck and held him aloft. The man's hands immediately gripped Adam's wrists as he struggled to break free. The sheer, delicious terror in the man's eyes made Adam squeeze all the more, then he plunged his fist into the man's heart, squeezing it within his ribcage. Ice expanded out the man's chest and ran its way over his body. Adam dropped the frozen form to the ground then proceeded down the street.

As people ran past and tried to maintain their distance, Adam shot forth beams of ice from his hands, each strike hitting its target with ice expanding and covering each person. It wasn't long before frozen mannequins of people filled the street.

Adam kept on.

In his head: *Tilmir. Phornifer. Grolinait.* The words thudded inside his frozen heart. What his master said, he must do.

A woman ran past, and Adam created an ice slide so he could slip in quickly beside her. He grabbed her by the shoulder and even from that holding point, lifted her off the ground.

She squealed.

He squeezed harder.

Soon, his frosty hold sent the ice over her, and she became like him: frozen and ready to comply.

All of them—each person on the street—would soon be ready to march on to spread and create a new species of man and ice.

Axiom-man headed down the hallway and, like the higher level, rooms ran off to either side, each one composed of merely plain ice walls. He had hoped for a clue of some sort: a symbol, an etching, something to give away who or what was responsible for this structure.

He saw his breath, and he knew if it wasn't for the thin, almost imperceptible light blue aura protecting him, he'd be cold.

Like the above floor, the hallway rounded to the rear of the ice construct. A large opening—like a gateway—loomed over him. Axiom-man touched down and stepped in, eyes fired up and ready for a fight should one occur. This room was huge but, like the others, plain except for a mound of ice in the middle of the room. Soon, Auroraman appeared opposite him.

"So?" Axiom-man asked.

"Bubkiss."

"Damn. I guess we just go back the way we came and head to Humboldt. Whatever made this might be on its way there, if it's not there already.

Eve kicked open the door to the Mom and Pop shop. The people huddled within all stared at her in collective awe. One person yelped. But only one. Eve smelled the fear and it only served to increase her sense of power. She went up to the man at the counter. He raised a trembling fist and for a brief second seemed to gather his courage because that fist came right at her a moment later. She let him strike her; he shouted when his hand broke against her frozen body. Clearly not giving up, the man swung at

FROZEN STORM

her with his other hand. She heard the bone crunch as his fingers broke against her jaw.

Someone ran for the door. Eve cut them off, placed both hands on their shoulders, and spread her icy goodness all over their body. She set aside the frozen woman and went after the next female in the store, this one small, half the size of the others.

"Mommy, what's wrong with her?" the little one asked. She was quickly quieted by an abrupt and short "Shh."

The moment Eve touched the child, the mother shrieked, "No! Not my baby!"

The woman came at Eve with everything she had. One hit; one hand broken. Another hit, yielding the same. A kick: broken foot. The woman hopped on one leg and used it to propel herself at Eve for one final blow. The woman cracked her shin against Eve's and she fell to the floor.

Eve knelt down before the child and took her by the hand. She placed the little one's hand on her mother's belly then, with a smile, spread the ice over them.

A loud bang rocked Eve's ears. She turned to see a man standing there pointing a rifle at her. He fired again; the bullet merely chipped her shoulder, her shoulder becoming whole again seconds after. She stormed toward him and ripped the gun from his hands. She then grabbed his face with her palm and sent his neck snapping backward. He dropped and froze over. She didn't know if he would return to life or not.

And she didn't care.

Tilmir.
Phornifer.
Grolinait.

Chapter Seven

Auroraman glanced over his shoulder to see Axiom-man trailing behind as they flew through the air. The cobalt hero seemed to have trouble keeping up.

"Am I going too fast for you?" Auroraman didn't have to see beneath Axiom-man's mask to know the man in blue grimaced.

"I can only fly so fast. Around two hundred kliks an hour these days," he said.

"That ain't too bad," Auroraman said, slowing down.

"Don't tell anyone."

"Who am I gonna tell?"

The two descended through the clouds and once Humboldt came into view, so did the half-completed wall surrounding it.

"This can't be good," Auroraman said.

"Did you really think it would be?"

Auroraman shot the other man a frown, then the two descended just outside the city to just outside the wall.

It stood what had to be thirty stories high.

Auroraman went up to it and felt the ice. It was the same as that of the ice structure: cold, harder than steel. Not that he expected anything different, but he had to know what they were dealing with.

"Axiom—" The man in blue was gone. Auroraman looked up to see Axiom-man at the top of the wall, seeming to be checking things over.

Axiom-man dove down and quickly landed beside him. "The wall is ten feet thick, possibly a dozen in some places. This thing isn't coming down."

FROZEN STORM

"Then we better stop what's making it before the whole city is surrounded."

"Agreed. Try and stick together if possible, but if we need to separate, so be it. Common meeting place?"

"City hall. It's—"

"I'll find it."

"Then let's move."

The two flew along the wall, using it as a guide. Whoever was in charge of this surely would be along it.

"Be careful," Axiom-man said.

"I will," Auroraman replied. He took note of the opaqueness of the wall. *Man, that thing is dense,* he thought. Heck, he even wondered if an energy beam from his staff would be enough to crack it. He was still learning how the staff worked and the limits, if any, of its power. Were the limits only those he beset upon himself, or were they of the staff itself? There was no way to know other than time and usage.

Something came into view below.

A man.

An . . . ice . . . man.

For a second, Auroraman thought it was the legendary yeti, but as he got closer and upon a keener inspection did he see it was humanoid. *Ice powers,* he thought. *Great.*

The man shot beam after beam of ice from his hands, constructing the wall. Auroraman wanted to believe this was someone good and all they were doing were testing what they could and could not do with the ice. However, he feared, that probably wasn't the case and then wondered if Axiom-man's cynicism was rubbing off on him.

The two landed beside the ice man.

"Hello there, I'm Auror—" A blast of ice went his way and struck him in the chest, sending him flying back in a stream of cold.

"Back off," Axiom-man said and flew at the man.

The man shot an ice beam at Axiom-man and sent him flying backward as well. Soon, sharp stakes of ice went forth from the man's fingers and punctured through Axiom-man's cape as he dodged to the side.

Auroraman went at the man again. Perhaps the fellow was scared. Perhaps this attack was merely self-defense. Perhaps—

More ice headed his way. Auroraman dodged the first blast, but was struck by the second, and soon found himself stuck beneath a sheet of ice so heavy he could barely make it move.

Axiom-man was quickly at his side. "Hold on." He gripped the ice sheet from underneath and lifted it off of him.

"Thanks," Auroraman said.

Axiom-man didn't reply and instead flew straight at the man constructing the wall. The man shot beams of ice at the wall and connected them to his hands, using the beams like tow-ropes. He yanked hard, and a portion of the wall toppled, landing on Axiom-man's leg.

Axiom-man yelled from the strike.

This time Auroraman was at his side. "I can blast it off."

"And tear my leg from my body in the process? No thanks." Axiom-man nodded toward the piece on him. "Together."

Auroraman bent down to grab the sheet and help lift it off his ally. A beam of ice struck him, waves of pain echoing throughout his chest. Though he didn't feel a crack, he thought a rib might've been broken or, at least,

FROZEN STORM

twisted out of place. It hurt to breathe. He shoved the pain from his mind and shot at the ice man with an energy beam from his staff. The blast hit the ice man and sent him a couple of steps back. He used the opportunity to help get the sheet of ice off of Axiom-man. The two worked together and were able to set it aside.

"Is it broken?" Auroraman asked. "Your leg?"

"No. I have an aura that protects my body. I'm not invincible, but it protects my body to a certain extent despite me still feeling part of the blow."

"Must be handy."

A ray of ice shot in between them, driving them apart.

Axiom-man fired up the energy beams around his eyes and shot at the ice man. The man moved, and Axiom-man missed. The ice man quickly retaliated and sent both Auroraman and Axiom-man flying back with two simultaneous bursts of ice. Then the man went back to work building the wall.

"This is getting pointless," Auroraman said.

"We have to beat him. Clearly, he means to harm anyone who gets in his way."

"Agreed, but he's stronger than us and, so far, my tricks aren't working."

Axiom-man took off full speed and tackled the ice man to the ground.

"Get off me!" the man said. "Get off . . . Crystallion!" Ice shot forth from the man's hands and sent Axiom-man into the air atop a pillar of ice. Axiom-man dove off it once it reached its apex. Using Crystallion's looking up as a distraction, Auroraman tackled him from the side and took him to the ground. He didn't know what happened but soon found himself encased in ice, unable to move, and unable to breathe.

Chapter Eight

Axiom-man had taken the ice-enclosed Auroraman far away from the scene. He couldn't tell from the blue of the ice if Auroraman himself had turned blue from either suffocation or hypothermia. He could only hope he wasn't too late.

He hammered at the ice with his fists, using all the strength he had to crack the exterior. Bit by bit, he chipped away at it, getting to his comrade beneath. This was no ordinary ice. Each strike sent a tingle up his arm, a sensation of fear he had always associated with the black clouds. Aside from his emergence here, it'd been a long while since he last felt the cloud's presence. Whatever made up this ice was somehow mingled with it.

Once again, he thought, *everything is my fault.*

He slammed away at the ice then stood back and shot his eye beams at the ice surrounding Auroraman's legs. It was slow-going, but eventually, he was able to get through. Auroraman toppled forward and hit the ground. Axiom-man rolled him over and put an ear to his mouth.

He wasn't breathing, nor was that big beard moving with any rise and fall of his chest.

Mouth-to-mouth. It was the only way. Axiom-man pulled down his mask, but still kept his powers activated so in case Auroraman awoke and looked at him, all the bearded man would see was a face with blue, crackling eyes and blue hair. Axiom-man started the chest compressions and blew air into Auroraman's lungs. He repeated it over and over. At first, the big man didn't seem to react, but after about a minute, he gasped with a huge lungful of air.

FROZEN STORM

Axiom-man quickly put his mask back in place.

"Thank . . . you . . ." Auroraman barely managed.

"Don't mention it."

Auroraman coughed and took in several big lungfuls of air before speaking again. This time the rhythm of his words was more normal. "That guy . . . Crystallion . . . he calls himself." He coughed. "He handed our butts to us."

"I know. He's strong."

"It's impossible."

Axiom-man couldn't believe his always-positive friend actually said that. "No, it's not. There has to be a way to beat him. Everyone has a weakness."

Auroraman nodded.

"I say we burn him down," Axiom-man said.

"No killing."

"That's not what I meant. Gather your strength. We have work to do."

Eve stepped through the streets, freezing everyone in her path: the old lady, the guy on the bicycle, the pizza delivery man. But it was too slow. She needed a mass of bodies, everyone in one place. She drifted inward. Something was there, something niggling at the back of her mind. She was smaller then, always looking up at the world. She was a child. Yes, she was a child. There were others like her, other children. They met nearly every day somewhere. Then she knew.

She knew exactly where she was going.

Eve created a platform of ice upon which to slide, the ice so hard and so slick it had no trouble gliding over the pavement, and the cold of her core kept it frozen and the obeyer of her every command.

Some of the people that were out cleared the way before her. Others stood stuck in one spot, shrieking. Eve grabbed a woman passing by and hugged her until she was frozen solid. She tossed her to the ground and kept riding. The building she looked for should be obvious. It'd be labeled. Suddenly, all of the names of the surrounding businesses came to life around her.

Laundr-o-mat. Store. Post Office. Drug Store. Burger Joint. Toy Store.

Then she found it.

School.

Eve smiled and slid up the front lawn and stopped at the doors. She reached out and took hold of the handles and flung the doors open. As she stormed down the hallway, the main doors swung shut, and she reached behind her and froze them closed.

The halls were empty, and she feared everyone had gone. Then there were small voices. Little ones lilting and laughing. She approached the first door on her left and opened it. Her mind—it was all coming back to her. This was a classroom—just like she used to go to when she was young. Everyone in the class stared at her. A couple kids laughed.

A man took cover behind a big desk.

Some leader, cowering like that, she thought.

Eve looked everyone over. These would be perfect. There were so many. At least twenty-five.

One came up to her, a little girl with blonde hair. "Are you a superhero?"

Eve stared down at her and looked her in the eye. "No, my dear. I am something much worse." She grabbed the girl by the shoulders and froze her solid. The kids screamed; some bolted for the door. Eve froze it shut.

FROZEN STORM

There would be no escape.

She pounced, working her way down the aisles, touching child after child after child. It didn't take long for the classroom to become a freezer with children frozen to their seats, some with their hands raised in panic. Children in mid-run. Children in mid-crouch, as if hiding. One even laying on the tiled floor.

The man still cowered behind his desk. Eve approached him and pulled him to his feet by his tie. "Poor soul, so scared." She gripped his jaw in her palm and sent a blast of ice through him. The man frosted over.

Eve charged for the door and ripped it open; the ice once sealing it peeled away at her will.

One by one each room would fall.

One by one each room would rise.

One by one they would release their spawn, frozen, frosty, and cold.

I need more, Adam thought as he released a teen from his grasp. He glanced across the street.

The Pioneer.

People.

Warm people that needed his touch.

He crossed the street, freezing the car and its driver heading toward him.

Adam entered the bar and sealed the door shut with a block of ice. Music blared. A—song?—he knew, somewhere, there, far away and deep within.

"T-N-T . . ." it came.

Eyes began to fall upon him, fear lacing some of them, others merely glazed over, and a few others keen and sharp. Those standing took a step back; those in their seats stood.

It was time to play.

A big man with a handlebar moustache and two skull-filled sleeves of tattoos came up to him. "Lookie, bub. This ain't no place for a costume."

Costume? He knew the word. Clothes. Right. It meant clothes. "This isn't a costume," Adam said and placed his hand on the man's shoulder. Immediately cold spread over him, ice cascading down his arms, crawling up his neck, freezing his feet to the floor. Soon, the placed was filled with cuss words and chairs scraping along the floor.

A couple burly guys with guts bigger than some men's chests came toward him. Adam crouched and shot forth a beam of ice from each hand, freezing the men.

Something hard shattered across the back of his head. He turned to see a woman holding a busted beer bottle, a stunned look on her face. Her white-blonde hair reminded him of snow. Adam placed both hands around her neck and froze her solid.

A wooden round table flew toward him like a flying saucer. He smashed down its middle with his rock-solid hand, splintering the thing in two, then stormed over toward the pair of leather-clad men who threw it. He picked up each by the neck and breathed on one and let ice flow from his fingers onto the other. He tossed the men away, marveling at his own strength. When the two hit the floor, their frozen transformation was complete.

And he'd had just about enough.

Adam positioned himself so he had a panorama of the whole room and spread ice and snow from his fingertips. The walls, floor, and ceiling washed blue and glistened white. People scrambled for the door, some slipping and sprawling out. The frozen door wouldn't budge. They faced Adam.

"This isn't a costume," he said. "*I* am not a costume."

He froze them all.

Chapter Nine

THE WORK, THOUGH slightly slow-going, was finally coming together. Crystallion stood back and gazed up at the wall he created. For a moment, he wasn't sure if he'd have enough time to contain everyone to create his world.

The whir of sirens filled the air as police cruisers rocked their way over the frozen grass toward him. They slid when they stopped. There was five of them. Then ten doors opened, each with an armed cop behind them, guns pointed at him.

They just don't understand, he thought. *I don't think they ever will. I am the one with the power. I am the one who lost everything then gained it all. It is my will that's done, not theirs. Never theirs. Never.* He chose to calmly stand before them. Let them think he was weak. Let them think they could dominate a god.

"Do not move," came a female voice over a bullhorn. "Put your hands up and turn around."

Crystallion heard the trepidation in her voice yet there was still some confidence. She seemed familiar with those with special abilities. She obviously knew about that guy with the beard and the staff. Did she know about Axiom-man? It was difficult to tell, but it didn't matter. However, he complied with her wishes and raised his hands and turned away from them. He listened carefully, then heard footsteps gently step across the ice.

Closer. Come closer, he thought. Crystallion waited. Someone said, "Whoop," no doubt after slipping. *Just keep coming closer.*

From right behind him, a gruff male voice: "Take off your mask or helmet or whatever it is that you've got on."

FROZEN STORM

"Do you think I wear a mere mask to hide my true face?" Crystallion replied.

He was met with no response.

"What you see is who I am. What you see . . . is something you are not acquainted with." He turned and faced them.

"We said turn around!" the man said and pointed the gun square at Crystallion's forehead. He adjusted the .9mm in his hand. "I'm not kidding around!"

"Neither am I," Crystallion said, then went to move. The gun went off, the bullet hitting him between the eyes. Its crushed form fell to the ice at their feet.

Crystallion grabbed the gun and kept his grip on the man's hand. Ice swam up the man's arm as he froze solid. The cop standing beside him stood there with mouth agape. Crystallion grabbed him by the shoulders and sent ice through the man's system.

Two frozen.

Eight left.

A barrage of gunfire sprayed his body, each bullet breaking against his rock-hard form. He held out his hands and froze the first two cops he saw.

Six left.

Another one kept stepping toward him, firing shot after shot, each bullet completely unfelt. Crystallion grabbed the man by the head then forced his mouth open and shoved his ice-cold hand into the man's mouth. As the man froze over, he ripped out his tongue. Once it froze in his hand, he crushed it between his fingers.

Five.

He held out his arms and blasted ice into the cop cars, sending them sliding across the icy field. One cop got caught in the line of fire and became a cold statue.

Four.

Guns reloaded. They rapidly fired shot after shot in a clear mad panic.

"Yes," Crystallion said. "I am your god now. I am the one with more power than you could invent or control."

He took a female cop by the throat, spun her around, and held her hostage-style but let the cold leak from his body, freezing her over.

Three.

Crystallion fired an ice shard from his fingers, embedding it in the nearest cop's gut. The ice spread over his uniformed middle and soon he was covered.

Two.

He blasted another cop, freezing him over.

The final cop stood there, bold, even brave. Yet . . . a coward. "You're not taking me," he said and held the gun barrel to his head.

"I am." Crystallion sent another shard forward, shooting the gun from the man's hand. He took the cop by the throat and pinned him to the ground. The man's eyes widened in terror. "I am ice," Crystallion said. "I am snow. I am winter. Freeze." Ice crawled and spread all over the man's body, his eyes frozen in panic, his last gaze that of fear.

Crystallion stepped away from the police and resumed work on his wall.

Soon it would be completed and then the city within would be his.

Axiom-man and Auroraman flew into downtown Humboldt, landing on Main Street. Up and down the road, cars were frozen to one spot, people trapped inside. On the sidewalks or in mid-stride along the crosswalks,

FROZEN STORM

people were frozen in place, ice sculptures of their former selves.

Auroraman stepped up to one, dipped his sunglasses, his heart sinking. It wasn't supposed to be this way. This was his beloved town, one brimming with peace and life. Now . . . now it was quickly becoming a frozen wasteland. This poor soul in front of him, a woman, perhaps in her mid-forties, locked in place, feet frozen to the ground, body covered in ice. He thought about smashing her free with his staff, but then thought better of it, thinking perhaps the effort to set her free would shatter her and kill her.

A loud pop followed by the creak of metal sounded behind him as Axiom-man busted open one of the frozen car doors and bent it forward over the ice coating the front of the vehicle. He had his hand out to the man and child within.

Auroraman pulled his sunglasses back up and joined the caped figure.

"It's going to be all right," Axiom-man said, pulling the man out of the car. The man quickly turned away after and dug for the child within. Once the toddler was free, the little boy clung to the man as if his life depended on it.

Probably does, Auroraman thought.

"Who are you?" the man asked.

"Axiom-man."

The man looked in Auroraman's direction. "Is he with you?"

Auroraman nodded.

The man swept his hand out, showcasing the frozen street and people. "What in the hell are you guys gonna do about this?" Then, quieter, "What can you do?"

"We're going to do all we can to bring Humboldt back from this. We're going to find the one responsible and—"

Axiom-man put a hand on Auroraman's shoulder, cutting him off. "What happened, sir?"

"Some woman," the man said. "At least, I think she was a woman. She just walked down the road as if out for a stroll, but out of her hands—ice, cold. Snow. I don't know how she did it or how she could even move being made out of ice herself, but she froze everybody and anybody that got in her way. Any*thing* that got in her way."

"Did you get a name?"

"What do I look like, a cop? No, I didn't get a name. She came right up to my car and froze the damn thing with me and my kid inside it. She looked as if she was gonna smash the window and get me for real but then turned the moment someone else came nearby and froze them solid. She seemed to have gotten distracted by everyone else out and about and took off, blasting ice every which way. Why the ice didn't spear right through people when it hit them . . . . You guys better do something and do it quick."

"We're going to," Auroraman said. Once more, he surveyed the street. *So many people either trapped or dead, encased in ice.*

"Again, like what?" the man said.

"Like set this town free."

The two flew off after telling the father and son to get to safety, preferably some place indoors and out of sight. Auroraman and Axiom-man paused, hovering above the town. Both glanced this way and that, trying to get an eyeful of the city below. Unfortunately, it had gotten so

FROZEN STORM

white and gray with snow and ice it was difficult to make out anything.

"We need to save those people," Axiom-man said. "The frozen ones."

"Are they able to be saved? They're not dead inside there?"

"We need to find out and set free as many as we can. We need to save lives. Then we go after the bad guy and take them down."

"Sounds like a her."

"What's that?"

"Nothing. Let's go."

The two raced back down toward the street.

The main road out of town was jam-packed with cars, horns blaring, everyone in a panic to get away from what was happening.

Perfect, Crystallion thought. He slid his way in between the cars and got to the fore of the line. "No one escapes."

He stretched out his hands, sending forth blast after blast of icy beams of frost. Ice quickly encased cars. He even went after the road itself, making it so slick that the finest of tires would have a hard time gaining ground.

Some people got out of their vehicles before he could get to them, so he chased them down with ice rays, freezing the people in place. Far down the line, closer to town, more cars were headed his way. Crystallion strode toward them, firing blast after blast of ice, then, two hands joined together, sent an enormous wave of ice, splitting the small lateral spaces between the vehicles, driving them apart and covering them in cold. With a scream, he let them have it. Cars started going up as if exploding . . . but not with fire—ice. The ground rumbled beneath them and mounds of ice began to form underneath the vehicles. Those still running fell to their knees from the shaking ground. Car alarms went off on those who parked and started to make a break for it. More horns blared, and in the cacophony of panicked traffic, Crystallion poured all his energy into his ice beams.

Cars rocked back. Some flipped over.

The ground grew, and his wall—

—his wall began to grow. At the mouth of town at first, then soon all over.

A grin formed on his face. *I can command the earth itself. The moisture in the ground and air—mine for the freezing.*

Crystals formed and coalesced above the wall's top, the thing growing taller and taller. Where there hadn't been a section of wall before, frozen earth rose from the ground and mingled with the water in the air.

People shrieked. Children screamed. He approached a family huddled together and sent a blanket of ice over them, silencing their cries, pausing them in frozen terror.

And the wall got bigger.

Chapter Ten

Everyone who received Eve's icy touch became a mannequin of frost and cold. She laid hands on everyone she could, making disciples for her master. To serve him, to please him—it was all that mattered.

This time she marched through suburbia, sending icy ball after icy ball through windows of houses and cars. Those who came running out to see what happened she quickly froze in place.

An old man sat on a bus bench. He must've been lost in thought because he didn't seem to notice her approach. He would freeze, too.

Eve raised her hand to lock him in place on the bench and let the ice flow. The old man froze over, not moving once from her icy attack.

She wasn't sure how many people her master wanted frozen, but she assumed he wanted as many as possible.

Tilmir. Phornifer. Grolinait. It rang her head like a command.

Eve kept walking.

Adam blew open the doors to the swimming centre with a blast of cold air. The lady working the greeting desk stared at him then, a moment later, screamed. He quickly silenced her with a blast of cold that entered through her mouth. She froze over, and he moved on to the others sitting in the lobby. A family sat huddled in the corner, cowering in fear. He blanketed them with ice and froze them in their family hug. A couple of elderly ladies shook and whimpered, and he silenced their sounds and frosted them over.

A little boy came up to him despite who was presumably his mother shouting, "Trevor! Trevor get back here!"

"Excuse me, Mr. Ice Man, what are you doing?"

Adam simply glared at him then gripped the boy by the top of his head and froze him over. The mother shrieked and quickly received a blast of cold to the face.

Through the window to his left, he saw the swimming pool. People swam and played and splashed about. Adam aimed his hands at the wall and iced the whole thing, freezing the wood and brick through and through. With a final cold gust of air, he sent the wall exploding out into the pool area. He moved forward, entering where everybody swam. Each set of eyes that set upon him led to that person scrambling to get out of the pool. Adam didn't care, and he blasted ice and cold into the swimming pool, quickly turning it into a skating rink and freezing the souls that hadn't gotten out of the water. People tried to escape but he had blocked the entrance.

One guy made a break for it. Adam froze him as an example to prove the people were his and there was nothing they could do.

Tilmir.

Phornifer.

Grolinait.

The phrase rang in his head.

Make disciples.

"Yes, Master," Adam said and took out those who remained standing. Each froze over in various positions, some standing erect, others crouching, a few passed out on the floor.

FROZEN STORM

Adam sprayed snow into the air then, satisfied with his handy work, left the pool and headed back toward the street.

Axiom-man and Auroraman stood in the middle of Humboldt. The whole town was lost, trapped inside a thick wall of ice, its citizens frozen over as cold, crystal-like mannequins.

"Everyone's dead," Axiom-man said.

"Maybe," Auroraman said.

"What do you mean 'maybe'? Everyone is frozen solid, encased in ice. They either suffocated to death or died of hypothermia. What you have here is a plethora of frozen corpses. Humboldt has become a mass grave for the frozen dead."

"We can free them."

"With what?"

"Build a fire. Use those laser eye things you got. Thaw them out."

"Only to reveal gray and frozen corpses within. The cold would preserve the bodies for a, hopefully, proper burial later, but that doesn't really matter right now. What matters is finding the one responsible and stopping them before they can cause any more damage."

"I can't let the people of the town die. Too many loved ones."

"Listen, they're dead."

"Listen, they're not."

Axiom-man didn't know what to say to that. There was clearly no reasoning with the man, and reason was what they needed right now. He caught Auroraman raise his sunglasses and wipe his eyes. Obviously, this town meant a great deal to him along with the people in it the same way Winnipeg meant a great deal to himself. Axiom-man understood the need to save a dying city and trying all possible avenues to do it despite how crazy some of those ideas might be.

"Fine," Axiom-man said. "We'll build your fire."

"Thank you," Auroraman said.

The two were about to get to work when Auroraman's staff went off. Its green glow bathed Auroraman's face. "It's talking to me." The staff jerked forward toward one of the frozen people. Auroraman followed its lead. He stood there for a long time, occasionally sweeping the staff up and down the person's body.

Axiom-man stepped up to him. "Anything?"

"They're alive. I can't tell how alive, but they're alive, thank God."

"Maybe a fire might be too dangerous."

"Not if we position them a safe distance away yet close enough the heat thaws them."

"Maybe." Axiom-man went up to a frozen woman clutching her purse. This had to be handled carefully. He lit up his eyes and slowly bathed her in blue energy, ever so slowly scraping away layer after layer of ice.

"What are you doing?" Auroraman asked. "I thought—"

"I thought it over again. This is faster," Axiom-man said. He coated the woman in as much blue energy as he could, but restrained the force of his blast so he wouldn't blow a hole right through her. His eyes beams produced heat, but it was more of an electrical heat than fire heat. Slowly, the woman came more and more into view. She was a brunette and wore a red dress with patches of frost up and down her body.

FROZEN STORM

Auroraman braced himself behind her then caught her when she collapsed. As he slowly lowered her to the ground, the woman began thrashing about, screaming. Auroraman laid her down then took a step back.

"Miss?" Axiom-man said. "Miss, are you all right?"

Her shrieks grew louder and louder, her convulsions completely out of control. Axiom-man thought it might be hypothermia and she shook from the cold. She slammed her fists into the ground and with uncanny strength shoved herself to her feet. With a loud scream, the frost on her body grew and grew until it completely covered her again.

"Now look what you've done," Auroraman said raising an eyebrow.

"No time for jokes," Axiom-man said.

"I wasn't joking."

The ice coating her was at least four inches thick, if not more.

Axiom-man's ears ached from her cries. "Miss?"

She pointed her hands in the men's direction and let fly icy beams of snow and ice from her hands. The two dove out of the way, each somersaulting to the side. The woman took aim again and once more fired at them both.

My beams didn't help, Axiom-man thought. *It just made it worse. And now she has . . . powers.* The next beam of ice that headed his way came with such speed and ferocity it hit him square in the chest, sending him flying backward.

As Axiom-man skidded across the ground, he saw Auroraman take to the air and, with a warrior's battle cry, came down on the woman with his staff. The blow dropped her to her knees, and she fell over.

"If finesse doesn't work, try brute force," Auroraman said.

"Gee, thanks," Axiom-man muttered.

Crunching sounds filled the air followed by loud pops and snaps.

Auroraman and Axiom-man looked over their shoulders.

The town was beginning to move.

CHAPTER ELEVEN

AURORAMAN'S HEART SANK. Here was the town he loved transformed into vicious ice monsters. Or ice people. He didn't know what to call them. All he knew was there were real live bodies under that sheet of cold and somehow their minds had been poisoned to become weapons of death.

The first came at him. He simply shoved them away, but when the next grabbed him from behind, Auroraman spun around and socked the ice-man in the face. Thank goodness for ultra strength and mild invulnerability otherwise he surely would have broken his hand. No longer distracted, his heart pumped into overdrive when a half dozen frozen men and women made their way toward him. He let them get as close as possible then slammed down his staff, embedding it in the ground and letting it send off a shockwave of green energy, blowing the ice monsters back.

From beside him, what sounded like metal crashing into metal. He looked; Axiom-man was at work punching the ice monsters back and letting those eye beams fly into his enemies. The blasts weren't strong enough to kill them, but carried enough power to send the monsters a safe distance away.

More closed in on Auroraman. Icy fingers touched his body. He took to the air and aimed his staff at the dozen or so that nearly grabbed him and sent off shots of green light, blasting the ice people away. He hoped that maybe asserting dominance would get them to lighten up—if they still had their intelligence, that was—and they'd back off. No go. Some jumped and swung out their arms in an effort to grab him.

Below, Axiom-man flew close to ground level, arms outspread, taking out the legs of the ice creatures, making them fall down. He then ascended and joined Auroraman.

"We can't keep this up. They'll just keep coming," Axiom-man said.

"Agreed," Auroraman replied. "We need to know their weakness or some method to restore them to human beings again. Permanently. I can't . . . I can't destroy them. Can't kill them."

"I feel the same way. It'd be a last resort and one we'd have to learn to live with."

Auroraman looked around. He saw the perimeter ice wall, keeping the people of the town in. "We could fly unaffected people out."

"One by one? It'd take too long."

"I can create a giant bubble for them through my staff and take them out in loads."

"It's a good idea, but to rally everyone together and keep them safe and cart them out—it's too much of a risk."

Auroraman thought about it some more. "You're right."

Axiom-man nodded.

Below, the horde of ice people stared up at them.

It began to snow.

Crystallion brought down the frost, manipulating the moisture in the air to descend on Humboldt in a snowfall. The more cold, the more ice, the lower the temperature,

FROZEN STORM

the better. Standing upon the wall, he watched with pride as his minions marched all over town.

Screams rose on the air.

The attack had begun.

Little Jimmy and his mother huddled close together in their basement in a nook beneath the stairs.

"It's the safest place we can be," his mother had said despite the nook not having a door.

He snuggled into her chest and took comfort in her arms around him. They seemed to chase away the fear of the screams of panic that permeated the walls from outside.

Jimmy's heart jolted when a loud thunk came from upstairs. His mother gripped him tighter.

"Shh," she said. "Not a word."

Jimmy pressed his lips together.

Thunk.

Pause.

Thunk.

Thunk.

Thunkthunkthunk—Smash!

"The door," his mother whispered.

Jimmy pressed himself into her bosom even tighter.

Footsteps. Upstairs. They were heavy.

Jimmy's heart picked up pace. "Mom?" he whimpered.

"Shh," she said. "Just stay quiet. Everything is going to be okay."

The footfalls above got closer and closer—then stopped.

The air turned cool and the warmth of his mother's arms disappeared despite her arms still being around him. Jimmy glanced up. Frost slowly crept along the ceiling, lightly at first, then the ice grew and grew until it looked like an upside down skating rink. With a violent crash, two men made of ice smashed their way through the floor and landed in the basement. Immediately, the two men locked eyes on Jimmy and his mother, and slowly approached them. One of them raised his hand and in a beam of snow and ice, froze his mother solid. Icy chills ran through Jimmy's body from her touch. This time, the other ice man raised his hands and the last thing Jimmy saw was blinding white ice heading toward him. The last thing he felt was paralyzing cold.

Dev Harvey had been a firefighter since he was twenty-three. He thought he'd seen it all over the past thirty years, but today, instead of an inferno, Humboldt had frozen over. He and his crew—four in all plus him—were already in position, hose hooked up to the fire hydrant. He only wished the hoses spewed flame instead of water, but he had to work with what he had. Perhaps enough force from the water would blast these guys to smithereens, end their growing reign of terror.

Two of his men had hoses—Chuck and Stew. Hank sat in the truck, ready in case they had to make a quick getaway. Brad worked the outside of the truck and made sure all was in order.

A horde of about a dozen ice people—men and women—came toward them.

"Let 'em have it, boys," Dev said. "Let's blow these frost people back to the frozen hell they came from."

FROZEN STORM

Chuck and Stew opened the valves and cold water shot forth, driving the horde back. The force of the water didn't take chunks off them or seem to break anything like Dev had hoped, but it kept the monsters at a distance.

"It's working, boys. Crank 'er up to full power," Dev said.

"You got it," Chuck said.

The force of the water increased, forcing the horde of ice monsters back. "Don't let up!" Dev said.

"Never!" Stew shouted.

Water flowed. The ice creatures were about forty feet away.

A crackling sound filled the air and Dev took notice that ice made its way up the water and headed straight for them. "Kill the flow! Kill it!"

Before Brad could shut the thing down, the long rods of ice from the hose flew up into the air then rapidly spun around and came toward them like helicopter blades, knocking their heads from their bodies.

Everyone had laughed at Nicholas Christos when he told them he was really Santa Claus. He was fifty-two.

"Just go back to your year-round Christmas home and play dress-up there," someone once told him.

But it wasn't dress-up. He was the real deal with snow-white hair and a long beard. He needed glasses, so wore round spectacles lower down his nose. His red coat and pants with white trim were what kept his overweight body warm during the winter months. Black boots and a black belt with a big ol' silver buckle finished the winter wear. When the snow descended on the town and everything froze over, he took that as his cue to grab his massive burlap sack, sling it over his shoulder, and head to the toy store where he worked and start filling it up.

He stepped outside and headed to the bus stop. One should be around shortly.

Minutes passed, then a half hour. Then a whole hour. No bus.

Nicholas thought about summoning his reindeer from the North Pole, but didn't feel much like waiting a couple of hours in the cold for them, so he began hoofing it through the thickening snow and headed toward the toy store. Up ahead, men and women made of ice began to gather around him from all sides, some coming from just down the street and others drifting in from in between the houses.

Elves. It'd been a long time since Nicholas had seen one—not since last Christmas, anyway—but still thought it strange they were made of ice instead of flesh and blood like him.

"Greetings, my friends," he said as they got closer. "Thank goodness you're here. Christmas has come early this year." He let out a jolly ol' laugh. "This is the year of two Christmases, I reckon. Come, my friends, let's bring goodwill and cheer to all."

The ice people closed in around him. One brought his fingers together in a point and stabbed it into Nicholas's chest, pulling away at the flesh and bone in what Nicholas presumed was an effort to get at his heart. Nicholas tried to speak, to scream, to gasp, but all that came out of his mouth was a stream of blood that ran down his stark-white beard.

Christmas, he thought and dropped to his knees. The ice person still had him and, finally, pulled Nicholas's heart from his body.

FROZEN STORM

Nicholas fell over and the last thing he imagined before he joined the North Pole in the sky was the red and white no doubt surrounding him was just like his coat.

Chapter Twelve

Gunshots rang out toward the end of town.

Axiom-man and Auroraman swooped in. The cops were having a go at it against the ice people. Each shot they took only nicked the hardened ice. Even the shots that hit the creatures dead on merely took a small chunk out of them, but that was it.

Axiom-man landed beside one of the cops, while Auroraman did the same to another.

Axiom-man put his hand on the wrist of the cop's armed hand. "You're wasting your ammo," he said. "The ice is so hard on their bodies it's like shooting at steel."

"Who are you? What's with the cape?" the cop asked. He didn't seem too pleased about some guy trying to be a hero in the middle of a crisis. "Where's Auroraman?"

Axiom-man nodded in his partner's direction.

The cop followed his gaze. "Phew. At least he's here. You should get out of here before you get hurt. And take that stupid costume off."

Did the cop not see him land from the sky? Whatever. The cop was probably in crisis mode and wasn't paying much attention to anything.

The ice creatures drew closer. Axiom-man took a quick glance at the squad and was disappointed there were only a handful of them. "Where are the rest of police?"

"Beats me," the cop said. "These guys were all I could round up. The others . . . I don't know. Maybe frozen. Maybe dead. Maybe . . . one of them."

Axiom-man took note of Auroraman readying his staff.

FROZEN STORM

The creatures weren't far off, maybe forty feet. Maybe less. Axiom-man let his energy beams fill his eyes and kept the power at bay.

Auroraman shot a stream of glowing green energy at the creatures. They stopped in their tracks and started to slide backward from the staff's power. Axiom-man began shooting off firepower of his own and made sure each blast from his eyes sent the creatures flying back.

With each hit, the ice creatures lost ground. Oddly, they didn't make a sound. Only took the strikes, fell back, and slid across the ground or went up in the air only to fall and hit the snow. They didn't shatter. They simply got up and continued their advance.

Axiom-man and Auroraman came round and stood in front of the cops.

Over a bullhorn: "Auroraman and—and . . . Blue Guy, get out of our way."

"They're wasting bullets," Auroraman said.

"That's what I told one of them," Axiom-man said. "Their effort is futile."

"Let's keep doing what we're doing."

Axiom-man nodded, and together they shot blast after blast at the ice creatures, breaking up the swarm and showing them there would be no more advancing on Humboldt.

"Get to safety," Auroraman shouted at the cops. "We'll handle this."

Axiom-man glanced over his shoulder at the same time the cops exchanged glances with each other. They fired more bullets, seemingly unwilling to listen.

"Take about thirty steps forward and hit those things hard enough to take them down. Don't kill them. I have an idea," Axiom-man said.

Auroraman gave him a small salute and ran toward the creatures.

Axiom-man took to the air and flew away from the cops about a dozen feet above ground level. He turned around mid-air and fired up the power in his eyes.

If they're not going to listen, I'll make them listen, he thought.

He flew and blasted the crap out of the ground at an angle, tearing up the snow and soil and created a wall between the cops and the creatures. Amid the curses coming from the other side of the wall and the occasional gunshot, Axiom-man stretched out his hands and flew in between two ice creatures and knocked them to the ground. He spun around and fired at another, then did another spin and took one more out.

Auroraman fired off glowing green energy in every direction and made sure the creatures couldn't get any closer.

Axiom-man punched the one nearest him then gave a kick to another. He flew into one more, taking it by the waist and flew it into a snowbank. Axiom-man got up, blasted the thing once more with his eye beams, then tore off and body checked one heading for Auroraman.

"Thanks," Auroraman said.

"Don't mention it," he replied.

Auroraman swung his staff like a baseball bat and cracked it against the head of one of the creatures before turning and zapping another.

Axiom-man grabbed the heads of two of them and slammed their heads together. The creatures staggered, then he sent them flying away with blasts from his eyes.

It went on for a good half hour if not more: punches, kicks, energy blasts, picking the creatures up then

FROZEN STORM

slamming them into the ground—but they made no progress.

At least the cops were safe, and Axiom-man hoped they'd had the sense to go back to the station or go home and get out of harm's way.

"We need another plan," Axiom-man said, catching his breath.

"Agreed," Auroraman said, inhaling a massive lungful of air and letting it out. His breath frosted on the air.

The sun was going down, and Auroraman let out a noticeable shiver.

"You okay?" Axiom-man asked.

"Fine. Just . . . cold." He paused. "Why aren't you freezing?"

"That small aura around my body. Keeps the heat in."

"Lucky you."

"Can't you create a bubble to put yourself in with that thing?"

"If I did that, I wouldn't be able to use it against our foes."

"Look, we drove them back, but they kept coming. We need to regroup, but do it quickly. Let's finally go build that fire of yours."

Auroraman smiled.

The creatures closed in.

The heroes flew away.

———

Outside the frozen wall east of Humboldt, Axiom-man assembled the sticks and logs while Auroraman planted his staff in the ground and erected a glowing green bubble around them. Axiom-man checked out his pre-lit fire. It was crude, but what stick assemblage wasn't? He gave the tiny twigs at the bottom a steady stream of blue energy from his eyes until they ignited. He kept at it until some larger sticks began to burn.

"You can let go now," Axiom-man said, nodding toward his partner's staff.

Auroraman didn't take his hand off his staff. "If I let go, our protection vanishes. I need to hold the staff in order to maintain the constructs."

"I see."

Auroraman gazed up into the night sky. "My family is in there, and I don't know if they're dead or frozen. I need to go see them."

"That's a bad idea."

"Please. I need to see—"

"I don't want to know their names. I understand where you're coming from, but we're here to do a job, and your family is one of three things right now: the creatures, dead, or, hopefully, alive and safe. If we go see them, there's a chance we'll be followed, and it could harm them in the end."

It was hard to argue with him, but Axiom-man was right. Auroraman merely nodded at what he said, though his heart hurt not knowing what became of his family. Not taking his hand off the staff, he crouched and duck walked a little closer to the fire. With the flames contained within the bubble, it was getting hot in there fast, never mind the construct filling up with smoke. He adjusted the construct so there was a small hole at the top about a foot across. The smoke started escaping through it.

"We need a plan," Auroraman said.

"We've been saying that a lot. We've already seen what these creatures can do up close. We also know they're near indestructible. I don't want to kill anyone."

FROZEN STORM

"We've been saying that a lot, too, and me neither." The warmth felt good even through his leather jacket.

"We need to take care of this tonight. No sleeping, and we're certainly not waiting until morning."

"I already knew that. No sense saying it."

Axiom-man shot him a look.

"Sorry. I'm just concerned for my family."

Axiom-man came over and put a hand on his shoulder. "They'll be all right. Somehow, somewhere, they're safe."

"Wish I could believe you."

"You have to believe me. If you lose hope about them, how long until you lose hope about Humboldt?"

The man had a point. "Keep believing, then."

"Keep believing."

The two remained there until Auroraman was good and warm. "Okay, time to embrace the cold."

"Time to end this," Axiom-man said, his words like ice.

Auroraman dissipated the bubble and the two floated into the sky, first Auroraman then Axiom-man.

Lights. Rising up over the south side of the wall.

Bright lights.

Chapter Thirteen

The two flew to the south side of the wall, and just outside its perimeter tanks and jeeps rolled up along with two choppers making their way to the ground.

"You do realize," Axiom-man said, "this just got a whole lot more complicated."

"Why? They're here to help."

"And get hurt. We need to tell them to go away, though I know they won't listen. The effort is appreciated, but we can't look out both for them and the entire town. Land forcefully. Show them your power."

The two came down hard out of the sky and landed so firmly they both crouched from the impact. They stood before a row of three tanks, a fleet of jeeps, and the two choppers behind, their blades still whirring. A man exited the jeep, decked out head to toe in army garb.

"What in the blazes is going on here?" the man shouted. "Not only do we have a national crisis on our hands, we have another pajama boy trying to be a hero."

"I take it they don't like you," Axiom-man said quietly to his friend.

"Not really, no. Seems they feel I'm taking away not just their job, but their sworn duty, and those, my friend, are two separate things, the latter of which is more important."

"Understood."

The man marched right up to them. "I don't suppose you two idiots had anything to do with this, did you?"

Axiom-man knew the man was right. They'd triggered this whole thing. The two didn't reply.

FROZEN STORM

"I'll take that as a yes," the man said. "General Tom Young, leader of the gang back there."

Axiom-man didn't like the military all that much. Last time he was summoned by them, they wanted him to go overseas and fight wars for them. He knew he needed to adjust his attitude because the army would be a powerful ally if they could both see eye-to-eye.

"What do you plan on doing, General?" Auroraman asked.

"Blast the hell out of that wall and get in there."

"Don't," Axiom-man said. "You breach that wall and the creatures contained within will spill out."

"Creatures?"

"Ice . . . creatures. Monsters. Killers. You don't want them getting out of the town."

"What exactly happened here?" the general asked.

Auroraman filled him in but left out the part about triggering the portal which led Axiom-man here along with this mess.

"I see," the general said once Auroraman was done. "Thank you." He turned and walked away.

Axiom-man let out a sigh of relief. "That went better than I thought."

"Yes, it did. It—"

The general shouted, "Light 'em up, boys!" Immediately, the tanks came to life and rolled forward, their cannons rising.

"No, don't!" Axiom-man shouted and flew to the nearest tank. Before he could grab hold of the cannon, the thing went off and he heard the deafening impact against the ice.

Auroraman set himself up in front of the other tank, but before he could, what Axiom-man assumed, do something, the cannon fired. Auroraman dove to the ground. The ice wall got struck.

The two tanks went at it, blowing hole after hole into the wall.

A half dozen men in uniform marched forward and positioned themselves in between the tanks. They broke off into groups of two. Out of those two, one of the men pulled out a missile launcher from behind his back, the other man crouching behind him to reload. They fired shot after shot.

Axiom-man didn't know what was going to happen next, but he had a sinking feeling the ice creatures would be drawn to the noise and, soon, there'd be chaos.

The moment the wall was breached, the ice creatures began to pour through the opening. Auroraman immediately jumped into action and planted his staff in the ground and created a green wall between the creatures and the military. He glanced over at the general and saw the look of disbelief on his face.

This is what happens when you don't listen, Auroraman thought.

Soon, the ice creatures began pounding on the green force field, their icy fists smashing into it. Auroraman felt each impact and, with each impact, focused even more on making the field stronger and stronger.

He looked to his left and saw Axiom-man take off into the air and land on the other side of the semi-transparent force field. Soon, the man in the blue cape's eyes lit up, and he blasted any creature that got near him. Auroraman noticed Axiom-man blasted the creatures further and further from the wall.

FROZEN STORM

Auroraman looked over his shoulder. The soldiers were gone, and the general had just finished mounting into a jeep. The vehicles turned—half of them to the left, half of them to the right—and made their way along the green wall until they reached its end. They rounded in front of the green wall and the men deployed, fully armed. In seconds, shots rang out on the air as the army fired shot after shot at the creatures. Some temporarily went down, but then got up with a vengeance and charged the soldier that attacked them. One ice creature tore the head off one soldier; another creature ripped the arms from another. A third ice creature stormed over to a soldier firing at it and held out his hands and covered the soldier in ice.

"No!" Auroraman shouted. He powered down the wall and leapt into the air and landed in front of the vehicles once more. This time he focused harder and created a thicker, taller wall, this one rounding the soldiers in a glowing green dome.

On the other side of the green, Axiom-man was on the ground, an ice creature wailing on him.

If it wasn't for the aura surrounding his body, Axiom-man would have been knocked out cold by now. Each blow from the creature's icy fists rattled him, but didn't crush his cheekbones or skull. He grabbed the creature by the neck and threw it off him. He sprang to his feet and zapped another creature coming toward him. One came in from the side and he kicked it away, then pushed off the ground and flew into another creature. He grabbed the creature by the leg and swung him around, knocking back other creatures coming toward him.

Amidst the chaos, he heard shouts coming from the other side of the green force field. His attention was quickly drawn to the creature he held and how it bent itself into two and tried biting his arm. He threw the creature into a handful of others coming toward him. The impact knocked the other creatures back.

But they still kept coming.

The whirring of chopper blades rang in Axiom-man's ears. He took a quick look inside Auroraman's protective bubble and saw the choppers beginning to rise. Once they hit the top of the bubble, their blades beat upon the green glow. Axiom-man glanced at Auroraman and saw his face twist into focused concentration. The green bubble held a little longer . . . then blew. Auroraman fell to his knees beside his staff. The choppers rose into the air and faced the onslaught of ice creatures. They opened fire, riddling the creatures with bullets. It didn't matter. Aside from chips of ice flying off them or the occasional one losing a limb, the ice creatures continued their advance.

"Retreat!" Axiom-man shouted at the soldiers. As if anyone heard him.

They continued firing until a blade of ice streaked through the air and sliced one of the choppers in two. The chopper spun as it broke apart and crashed hard into the ground. The same thing happened to the second chopper, and it went up in a blaze of fireballs.

Axiom-man was about to fly to assist anyone that might be trapped inside when he heard footfalls on the ice behind him. He turned around. An entire battalion of ice creatures led by a larger male one came marching toward him.

Chapter Fourteen

Adam knew that whoever these two were, they could only spell trouble. Unlike the other warm bodies out there, these two were special—like him. And they were special enough to kill.

The one with the staff with a glowing globe on its end flew toward them first, getting himself right into the thick of it. He began swinging his staff this way and that, striking anything icy in his path. Each creature that came toward him went up in the air with each blow. Without warning, green beams of energy came spewing forth from the globe, zapping the creatures and keeping them at bay.

Adam raised his icy hand, morphing it into a sword, and charged just as the one in the blue cape came flying toward him. The man in blue dodged the first swipe of the blade and the second, but the third punctured a hole in his cape and the fourth sliced across his middle just he jumped backward. For some reason, the frozen sword didn't cut through the man. Didn't even leave a mark.

Adam quickly glanced over at the others in his army. Some attacked the soldiers, while others took on the guy with the staff. With a powerful blow, the man planted his staff in the ground and let green energy permeate the area. Sharp ringing cut through Adam's ears and his insides shook. He dropped to his knees.

"Whatever you're doing, keep doing it," the man in blue said.

The other ice creatures put their hands to their ears and stood there vibrating.

"I'm harnessing the audio waves on the air, making them all sound at once and trying to route them so they avoid you and me," the man with the staff said.

Adam glanced over at the man who just spoke. The man's arms shook as he held fast to his staff.

That was the key.

The staff.

Adam forced himself onto his feet. The man in blue went to take a swing at him, but he blocked it with the broadside of the sword, leaving the man to cradle his forearm. Adam ran toward the man with the staff and tackled him to the ground. The ear-piercing sound ceased, and Adam could finally think straight. He needed to make this guy like him: an ice man. He reached out to touch him but a light green force field surrounded the big man with the long beard.

Like a battering ram, something hit him from behind. The man in blue had him around the waist and flew him through the air at ever-gathering speeds until launching him backward to sail through the air and crash into the side of a building.

Axiom-man flew back to the action to help Auroraman. Just as he arrived at the man's side and kicked away an ice creature, the globe atop Auroraman's staff began to glow then quickly turn dark as black pools of smoke filled the globe. From the top leaked a black cloud.

"I think this is your ride," Auroraman said.

Axiom-man looked around. The ice creatures were closing in.

FROZEN STORM

This was it. Finally. A portal. A way home. A door back to his world where he could finally put a stop to Redsaw's reign of terror and death. His world needed him. He had to go. The cost of life there could be in the millions, perhaps even billions if all bowed before Redsaw.

"Go!" Auroraman shouted.

Axiom-man blasted away two ice creatures with the energy beams from his eyes. "What about you? Humboldt?"

Grim determination washed over Auroraman's face. "I'll fight. I'll fight until I die. If the city is going to fall, I'm going to fall with it."

Axiom-man looked at the portal . . . then at the ice creatures. He could almost hear Redsaw laughing in the back of his mind.

He punched another ice creature and took the legs out from another. A third he sent flying back with yet another blast of energy from his eyes.

"Get. Out. Now," Auroraman said.

Axiom-man took a step toward the portal—then took a step back.

Not now.

Not tonight.

Not with a city about to perish.

The black cloud began to dissipate.

"Go, you idiot!" Auroraman shouted.

Axiom-man stood, feet planted.

It was time to get back to the fight.

He flew toward two creatures and grabbed them both by the waist but not before glancing back over his shoulders and watching his only way home disappear.

With an animalistic cry, Auroraman went to work blasting more creatures, and with a cry of his own,

A.P. FUCHS

Axiom-man shoved the creatures he carried forward, sending them both into frozen-over parked cars.

The snow quickly came down in big fat flakes and the winds picked up.

The big ice creature he had disposed of earlier ran toward him. Axiom-man planted his feet and let the creature have it with his eye beams.

The creatures slowly began to back off, at first a couple, then more. The big one didn't seem too pleased, especially after Axiom-man's eye beams drove it to its knees.

Are we winning? Auroraman thought. *Finally. Progress.*

He leaned his forehead against his staff and said a quick prayer of thankfulness.

It could be over. Finally over.

No.

Footsteps. Hard footsteps crunching on snow. Faint at first, but quickly growing louder. Auroraman gazed past Axiom-man and the immediate ice creatures and saw a woman made of ice calmly walking toward them, a legion of ice creatures following her.

To his left and right, Auroraman heard weapons readying. The remaining soldiers had come to his aid, and without waiting for permission, opened fire on anything frozen.

The bullets nicked and chipped at the creatures, but didn't do any lasting damage. Quickly, the entire ice battalion in front of them charged forward. The ice woman jumped into the air and landed hard in front of Auroraman.

FROZEN STORM

"And who might you be?" Auroraman asked, hoping she wouldn't attack.

"I am Eve. I am your destroyer." Her voice was cold, raspy. Frosty.

"And the man?"

"Adam, forged by the ice god Crystallion. Now, peasant, bow before me."

Was she serious? He didn't bow before anyone, especially not to her or, perhaps, this so-called god she'd mentioned. "No," he said.

"Then perish." Eve reached forward and picked Auroraman up by the neck. Her icy fingers slowly began to squeeze until he couldn't breathe.

He tried prying away her fingers, but their frosty hold wouldn't let up. When his words came out, they were barely audible. "Some . . . help . . . please?"

Axiom-man swooped in from the side and did a flying kick to her middle. The force of the blow knocked her away . . . taking Auroraman with her. The two skidded along the ground, then stopped. Auroraman got up, catching his breath, while Eve got to her own feet. Just as she was about to grab Auroraman again, he blocked her attack with his staff. Frost began to spread out from her hands and cover the staff. Auroraman held it firm and concentrated, forcing the frost back toward her fingers.

Come on, he thought. *Puuush.*

He yanked the staff away then shot a green beam of energy at her. Immediately after, he was airborne and started firing at the ice creatures from the sky. Axiom-man flew up and joined him, and together they shot blast after blast of energy at the creatures. Below, the remaining soldiers opened fire and the echo of gunshots crashed through the air. It was a futile effort. They were soon overrun.

"We can't keep this up forever," Axiom-man said. "We need to come up with a plan that will actually stop them."

"The wall is breached. We need to contain them."

"Agreed."

"I'll try to round them together and drive them back within the town. Can you build a wall?"

"Not an ice one, but I can use my eye beams to tear up the ground and create a kind of tidal wave of dirt. It's the best I can do."

"That's fine. Then make it as high as you can."

Auroraman flew past him and hovered in position in front of the ice creatures. He fired shot after shot, slowly but surely driving them back. He landed before them with a thud and slammed his staff into the ground, creating a shockwave of green energy that drove them back even further. Auroraman fired some more, then hit the air again and came back down, blasting more energy at the creatures. He did it over and over, pushing them back with a wild current of power. Behind him, he heard a whoosh then the violent tearing up of the earth as Axiom-man got to work doing his part.

Auroraman blasted the creatures again. And again. And again. The sound of the wall going up behind him was almost deafening. He glanced over his shoulder. A massive mound of earth that ran the span of the breach plugged the hole. From the other side, bright blue light hovered on the air as, presumably, Axiom-man flew back and forth up its length, digging up more and more dirt and making it higher.

Finally, the tearing of earth stopped and Axiom-man landed beside him. "Done."

"Good," Auroraman said. "Nice going."

"You, too."

FROZEN STORM

The creatures had been driven back some hundred feet away from them. It wouldn't take them long to reach Auroraman and Axiom-man and they'd yet again be dragged into battle with creatures they couldn't stop.

The ice woman led the creatures.

"Who is that?" Axiom-man asked.

"She calls herself Eve and she insisted I bow before her. No way, no how on that one."

"Is she the cause of this?"

"I don't know. But she has a partner. Adam."

"Adam and Eve," Axiom-man said quietly to himself, "which suggests that maybe someone even more powerful is behind this. If you want to get biblical, I mean."

"I have no issues with the Bible."

"Then we need to see if the theory is true." Axiom-man gave Auroraman a nudge and the two floated upward just as Eve and her army drew in.

Chapter Fifteen

"First thing, though, is we need to see the state of the town," Axiom-man said. "Can't leave civilians under attack."

"A little late for that, don't you think?"

"Ha. Ha." This wasn't a time for jokes, though he doubted Auroraman meant it that way.

As the two flew through the air over Humboldt, all Axiom-man saw below was white. The snow had landed thick and deep, with cars buried halfway up their doors or more.

He flew down closer; Auroraman followed his lead. There. A red Hyundai with people trapped inside. Axiom-man landed before it and immediately got to work thawing the ice. Auroraman went for the door once the ice was gone and let out the previously-trapped woman and child.

"Th-thank y-you," the woman said through chattering teeth. She scooped up the child and cradled him close to keep him warm.

"You two better find a place to get inside," Axiom-man said.

"Here, let me help you find somewhere," Auroraman said, and with a nod to Axiom-man, picked up the woman and child and flew them off to elsewhere in the town.

Axiom-man surveyed the area. The blinding snow blowing through the air made it nearly impossible to see. He rose up above the snow and flew up and down the length of the street, checking to see if anybody else needed help. Down and to his left, a cop smashed a

FROZEN STORM

window in the door to a bar with his elbow. Only when Axiom-man got closer did he see the cop was escorting somebody inside. It was good to see the peacekeepers doing their job.

Axiom-man landed beside him. "Officer."

"Who are you?"

"I'm called Axiom-man. I'm here with Auroraman and we—"

"Where is Humboldt's guardian?"

"He's gone to take someone to safety. I wanted to check in with you to see how you and the rest of the force are faring."

The cop seemed to make sure the person he just nudged inside the bar was out of earshot. "I don't know where they are. Dead, possibly, or maybe turned into those creatures. I've been alone for a couple hours already. All I'm trying to do is help where I can."

Axiom-man nodded. "Thank you for your service."

The cop nodded back. "Thank you for yours even though I don't know who you are. For all I know, you could be the one responsible for all this."

"Trust me, I'm not."

"Those are just words." The man's eyes suddenly went wide and he pulled out his gun.

Axiom-man turned around, eyes filled with power, ready for any creatures that might be encroaching on them. There was nothing there. He turned back to the cop. The gun was trained right on him. Axiom-man raised a hand and powered down his eyes.

"No sudden moves!" the cop said.

"I'm not trying to hurt you or anyone else. I'm trying to help."

"I'll kill you, I swear." Panic flashed over the cop's eyes. Axiom-man noticed the man's lips were blue. The panic was only natural.

"Please, listen to me. I'm here to help. I'll also leave you alone to prove my point." At least, he hoped it would. Axiom-man rose into the air. Just then the gun went off and the bullet nicked his ear. The warmth of blood trickled down his skin. Though his aura was strong, it wasn't fully bulletproof, and anything at point-blank range would do him in. Quickly, he sped into the sky in search of Auroraman. He found him standing in front of a school.

Axiom-man landed beside him. "All is well?"

"Seems so."

Axiom-man glanced toward the school. It was completely iced over. He hoped any kids inside were all right, and being indoors was the best place they could be. "Hey," he said, giving Auroraman a nudge. "You all right?"

It took a moment for Auroraman to respond. "Just thinking about something from my other life."

"I understand that. Life before the costume."

"In a way."

Axiom-man didn't pry any further. "We need to get going. We need to find the 'god' of all this."

Auroraman stroked the length of his beard. "This needs to end."

"Then let's go."

The two flew over and past the wall. Below, the army had been overrun. What could they have done against

FROZEN STORM

bulletproof enemies? Options were limited, if there were any at all.

"So much death," Auroraman said.

"Which is why it's so important we put a stop to this once and for all."

"I'm cold."

"Do you need another fire before we do this?"

Auroraman couldn't believe Axiom-man asked the question. "Are you kidding?"

"I just want you at your best."

Auroraman gripped his staff hard and flew ahead of him. "I'm always at my best."

The ice structure came up quickly, and the two landed before it.

"Someone's been busy," Axiom-man said.

The ice structure was no longer a simple one; it was an elaborate castle. From down here on ground level, there seemed to be an outer wall made of ice. Auroraman kept an eye out for sentries, but didn't see any.

"I suggest one quick sweep of the perimeter and then up and over," Auroraman said.

"Let's do it."

The two rose off the snow and flew around the wall; all four sides were identical, even constructed as such there were gaps on the top level as if a place to wage an attack. There was no one guarding the outside. Auroraman took the lead, and the two flew over the wall. Below, ice creatures, crystal-like humans guarding a ten-storey castle filled the courtyard.

"We need to find a way in without engaging," Axiom-man said.

Auroraman nodded. The two flew around the castle, varying their heights to make sure they missed nothing. The place was sealed up like Alcatraz.

"If we go down . . ." Auroraman said.

"We'll have no choice but to fight," Axiom-man said.

They rounded to the front of the castle where a giant ice door waited for them. It had two sides, each side at least eight stories tall. Below, ice creatures filled the base of the entrance.

"If we can open it from up here . . ." Auroraman said. He shot a blast of green from his staff. It struck the ice but didn't break through.

"Cut and pry. Hope you're strong enough," Axiom-man said.

"I might be, and if not" —he raised his staff— "this thing is."

Axiom-man flew in front of him. His eyes crackled with blue energy and he let loose, cutting in between the doors. As he worked, he moved up and down its height except for where the ice creatures guarded it below. Some tried to reach up and touch his boots or cape, but failed in their grasp. Axiom-man flew up, down, seeming to give it all he had. By the time he powered down, he'd managed to cut a three-inch-wide seam between the two doors.

Auroraman and he both flew up to it and each took a side.

"Ready?" Axiom-man said.

"Ready," Auroraman replied.

The two each gripped a side of the door and pulled.

And pulled.

When that failed, they pushed, grunting and groaning, putting every ounce of muscle they had behind it. The door didn't open.

"Stand back," Auroraman said. "Er . . . fly back."

Axiom-man obeyed and Auroraman's staff lit up.

Chapter Sixteen

Axiom-man quickly hovered back with a jolt. Two claws resembling the Jaws of Life burst forth from Auroraman's globe and wedged their way into the crevasse Axiom-man had created. With a focused grunt, Auroraman worked his staff and began to pry the giant ice doors open. The more the jaws wedged their way in, the wider the opening grew until the jaws found full purchase on the doors.

"Stay back," Auroraman said.

Axiom-man floated a little bit away.

Auroraman pulled with all he had and the giant ice doors collapsed outward, raining down on the creatures below. Axiom-man knew it wasn't intentional, but his heart ached at the loss of life. He glanced below and saw that some of the ice creatures had avoided the raining debris.

Now a giant hole stood at the top of the doors, the bottom two thirds or so still intact.

"Now we have a way in," Auroraman said.

"No kidding. Good work. That staff is pretty incredible."

"It can be."

They floated into the castle. The foyer below was similar to the way it had been when they first entered the place, but it was more elaborate and ornate, as if someone had taken the time to carve it out so it was regal despite being made of ice. On either side of the stairs leading to a horizontal hall at the top was a pair of identical statues of a man. He was made of ice, with details outlining what looked like a kingly robe, gloves, and boots. He even wore a crown. Axiom-man doubted it meant there were two of these people in here, but he felt this "king" was who they would be looking for. Then he realized it was the same man they'd encountered before.

Below, the foyer crawled with ice creatures. If the two heroes kept to the air, they would avoid most of them.

"We need to split up and find this guy once and for all," Axiom-man said.

"What about the buddy system?" Auroraman asked.

"Buddy system be damned. We can cover more ground if we split up, each take a wing. This place has clearly changed since we were last here and there's no guarantee the path to our man has stayed the same or is the same or anything like that."

"Fine. You go right. I'll go left."

"Done."

"Man, that's a long hallway," Auroraman said once he stepped foot in it. He got his staff ready. Far down the hall were the sounds of ice scrapping on ice and the distant calls of what could only be the ice creatures.

Swallowing his fear, Auroraman stepped toward them, going over in his head how he could defend himself without killing the creatures. His staff enabled him to construct nearly anything he wanted, but he was also a novice at it and could only think of rudimentary weapons to get a job done.

The creatures appeared and moved toward him. Auroraman focused and created a giant, green shovel construct and scooped up the majority of the creatures. He focused again and the shovel curved in on itself, creating a bubble. With the bubble tethered to the staff,

FROZEN STORM

Auroraman slammed the bubble against the dense ice walls, jolting the creatures within and causing some to slam against each other. He did it again against the opposite wall, then struck the ceiling, then, finally, the floor. The creatures within were clearly dazed.

Auroraman released the construct and ran past them to the next set of creatures beyond. One he clubbed hard against the head with the staff. Another he flipped over his shoulder and made it crash down in a heap. A quick rear stab with the staff to stave off another one, and a swat to the head of another to buy himself some distance.

The creatures kept coming.

Auroraman planted his staff. Focusing, he created a horizontal windmill. The blades? Baseball bats. He set the thing in motion, every ice creature that came near him clocked across the head. Auroraman used the defense as a means to get further down the hallway to the turn at the end.

Ice doors opened, and more creatures came out.

Surrounded, Auroraman floated above them and transformed his construct into a giant golf club and let the creatures have it with a mighty drive. He sent them flying and was able to get himself near the end of the hallway. Another creature came at him and grabbed the staff. Wrestling with him, Auroraman used his mighty strength and threw the creature clear across the hallway. Now, finally at the end of the hall, Auroraman turned a corner only to be greeted by more creatures.

He held the staff horizontally and transformed it into a giant bar with glowing green weights at the end, the kind you'd find in a gym. He then bench pressed his way down the hall, pushing back the creatures. Once he got them a fair distance down, he aimed his staff at the ceiling and manifested a dark green storm cloud. Thunder and lightning snapped and crashed into the crowd, and soon lightning bolts streamed out, each one cracking at a creature and knocking it down.

How these things are ever going to return to normal, I have no idea, he thought.

He kept the storm above his head and went further down the hall.

No doubt there would be more trouble, and he'd need to be ready.

The ice creature jumped on Axiom-man the moment he turned the corner into the hallway. Axiom-man wrestled him off him and tossed him against the wall.

I can't hurt these people, he thought. *Beneath the ice, they're still human.*

The creatures started coming at him. He flew up and over one and pushed the creature into another. Another creature came in from the side and Axiom-man grabbed its arm, spun it around, and hurled it into the wall. The force of the impact stunned the creature and slowed it down, just like Axiom-man had hoped.

Four more creatures moved in. Axiom-man flew over one and pushed it from behind, sending it sprawling across the floor. Out of the remaining three, two grabbed his arms. He brought his arms together and slammed the creatures' faces together. They dropped. The third came in with a swing. Axiom-man ducked and punched the thing. It was enough to send it staggering back a few steps. Powering up his eyes, Axiom-man glanced at the wall. He blasted the wall just to his left with everything he had. The wall crumbled down, creating a barrier between him and the creatures.

FROZEN STORM

Axiom-man flew on.

More creatures swarmed in, each trying to grab at him as he flew overhead. He landed, and each one that came near he pushed into the nearest wall. Stunning them was all he could do. He punched one. Kicked another. Just kept his strength restrained so as not so punch right through the things.

Once more, he blasted the wall, this one on the right, and created another barricade. Then he cursed himself for not thinking ahead, not thinking they might have been load-bearing walls and he could have brought the whole place down. Then again, with everything made of ice, it was hard to say how the construction of this place worked.

Axiom-man kept on the move.

He hoped Auroraman was doing the same elsewhere in the castle.

Auroraman had no choice but to go right. He passed underneath a set of doors, and the moment he was through, an ice door slammed down from the ceiling, taking away his exit. He stood at the beginning of a hallway, the walls of ice on either side polished to a shine. He brought up his staff and powered it up. If there were any creatures in here, fighting quarters would be tight. He walked down the hallway, each reflection he passed a parody of himself. Some were tall and skinny, others short and fat, others elongated hourglasses, and some as if his torso was a giant egg with tiny legs, hands, and head. He followed the hall to another right turn, then a left, then a right. The hallway came to an end, and he had a choice to go left or right. He held his staff aloft and concentrated, hoping the staff would guide him the right way.

He turned right and was relieved the staff hadn't led him to more hallways, but dismay washed over him at the sight of more ice creatures. He transformed the end of his staff to project giant saw blades and used those to cut away at the side walls and then, using its tractor beam, brought the walls in and down to trap the creatures so tightly together they couldn't even move.

Auroraman flew over them to the other side and entered a new hallway, this one with a spiral slide.

Well, might as well, he thought and sat down. *Whatever you do, don't drop the staff.*

Auroraman went down the slide.

Down, down, down.

CHAPTER SEVENTEEN

ALL THAT WAS missing was the carnival music. In front of Axiom-man was a merry-go-round, each animal on it made of ice, each pole running through them the same. The merry-go-round was so big it took up all the space in the room, and the only way to the other side was to go through it.

Cautiously, Axiom-man stepped onto the merry-go-round, found his footing on the ice, then proceeded past an elephant with one foot raised, a tiger in mid-pounce, a horse at a full gallop, and a gorilla positioned on all fours.

A rough grinding sound grew from beneath him, and the merry-go-round began to turn, slowly at first, then faster and faster until the thing was spinning so fast the exit on the other side rapidly passed by over and over.

Stomach beginning to spin with the merry-go-round, Axiom-man dropped to his knees and began punching at the base of the giant pole in the middle, the goal to reach whatever was turning this thing. All his mind's eye saw were icy gears turning.

He smashed through the floor, and before he could blast at it with his eye beams, the gorilla sprang to life and jumped on his back. Thank God for ultra strength otherwise he would have been crushed.

Axiom-man went down under the gorilla's weight. He flew out from underneath him and got the high ground by getting on the gorilla's back and sent an energy beam in between the thing's shoulder blades. The gorilla stood, reached around and grabbed him, then sent him hurtling against a merry-go-round pole. The pain raced down his spine and settled in his lower back. Axiom-man lunged at the gorilla and fired at it again, this time in the chest, then flew straight at it, pushing it through the nearest bar then back around into the elephant. The two collided and an icy squeal came from the elephant's trunk. It wrapped its trunk around Axiom-man, lifted him up then slammed him down. The gorilla pounced, but Axiom-man rolled out of the way. Having enough, he lit up his eye beams and zapped all the merry-go-round poles, including the one in the center. The top of the merry-go-round dropped and Axiom-man caught it. He then got to work quickly blasting it into smaller chunks, letting them land between him and the animals.

Over in the corner was a door. He threw the ice over his head and went through it.

Auroraman emerged in a small hallway that only accommodated his height and width, as if the narrow passage had been made for him. Along the floor were ice tiles with writing on it in a language he didn't understand.

But his staff would.

He shone the light of his staff on the ground and, when illuminated, the hallway appeared as if it was made of green, glowing crystals.

Auroraman stepped forward and the ice broke beneath his feet. He pulled his foot back.

So much for just walking, he thought. He couldn't fly either. The top of his head scraped the ceiling of this passage. He shone the ball at the end of his staff on the ground again. The language swirled and changed and arrows appeared, showing which tiles were safe.

Auroraman followed that path and made it to the other side, curious as to what was beyond the next door.

FROZEN STORM

The next room Axiom-man entered was empty. Cautiously, he walked across it, ready to take flight at a second's notice. A low rumbling filled the place, and the walls on either side of him began to close in, and fairly quickly, too. He ran to the end where the exit was and smashed his fists against it. He made a few crushed dents into the ice but had to outstretch his hands because the walls were coming in so close. The walls reached his palms and pressed against him with such force he wasn't sure if he could hold it.

Come on, he thought, *stand strong.*

Arms shaking, he kept the ice at bay.

He lit up his eyes and fired at the exit in front of him, giving it all he had to blast it away. Once he got through, he said, "One . . . two . . . three!" And dove forward and through the door just as the walls slammed together. He landed in a somersault then got to his feet.

Auroraman was in this next room with him. It was empty and narrow, some six feet wide by a dozen feet long. Axiom-man tried not to give any attention to the sudden feeling of claustrophobia.

"You made it," Auroraman said.

"So did you," he replied.

"I already checked the walls. Aside from the doors that dumped us in here, there aren't any others."

"A dead end."

Just as Auroraman nodded, a deep voice came from the ice surrounding them. The two suddenly got on guard, fists and staff raised.

The voice said, "You foolish, foolish mortals. You come to a place and see only what's in front of you. You miss what might be right in front of your face."

Not likely, Axiom-man thought. *I've been at this long enough to know things aren't always what they seem. Whoever's speaking, clearly they have an ego.*

"I am omnipresent in the snow. I am the ice. I am the cold." The small room shook—the walls, the floor, the ceiling—and the wall in front of them came crashing down, revealing a man made out of ice sitting on a throne. "I am Crystallion."

The man was huge, probably near seven feet when standing, and looked to weigh around two-fifty. The chair he sat upon was large, with curved ornamentation on its top and giant, beautiful snowflakes at the end of the armrests. A small set of stairs led up to a small platform in front of the throne.

"You two have tried to stop what I am creating, but what have you accomplished?" He paused. "Nothing. All you've done is defend yourselves and a small few others from my army. You didn't even try and end my people for good, but instead preserved them for fear of extinguishing the life within them. My life. Who the humans once were are now gone."

Adam and Eve appeared from behind the throne and stood by Crystallion's side, Adam on the right, Eve on the left.

Axiom-man looked to Auroraman, and before he could silence him, Auroraman said, "Undo what you have done. Return the people of Humboldt to what they were."

Crystallion merely shook his head in dismay. "You haven't heard a word I said. My life is now in them. They are one with me."

FROZEN STORM

"Then undo the connection," Auroraman said. "Set them free."

"For what? So you two can claim heroship and be the town's saviors?"

"No," Axiom-man said. "So that their lives can be preserved."

"This will not happen and you cannot force me." The room shook again and his throne and platform moved back, taking him and Adam and Eve along with it. Once at the far side of the now-enormous room, the ice on the walls to either side cracked, and for a second Axiom-man thought Crystallion was going to let them crumble down and act as a barrier between him and them. Instead, ice creatures poured out and lined up in front of Crystallion, facing Axiom-man and Auroraman. Adam and Eve then rounded to the front of the battalion, their faces cold and hard—no mercy.

In such a full room, there'd be no place to easily maneuver. And if Crystallion wasn't lying about him inhabiting the creatures, then there was no way Axiom-man and Auroraman would kill the monsters.

Axiom-man nodded at Auroraman and did something he knew he shouldn't do: Turn his back on his enemy.

Auroraman did the same.

"I'll make it quick." Axiom-man explained his plan to him then the two turned around. Their opponents had remained as they were.

"Last chance," Auroraman said. "Release the people."

Crystallion leaned forward on his throne. "Never."

Axiom-man nodded at Auroraman.

It was time.

Chapter Eighteen

Auroraman got into action and focused on his staff. He swept it across the room, gathering up the ice creatures in a containment bubble. The moment Adam and Eve saw what he was doing, they began running toward him. Above, Axiom-man used his energy beams to cut through the icy ceiling to create an opening for Auroraman to get the creatures outside. Adam changed course and created an ice slide upward toward Axiom-man, who flew back and forth across the ceiling as he tore it apart and brought it down on top of Crystallion and his throne.

Eve grabbed Auroraman from behind. He floated into the air, pulling on his staff to drag the glowing green bubble filled with ice creatures with him. She put him in a choke hold and it took all he had to tighten the muscles around his neck and resist the pressure.

"Time to die, little beard," Eve said.

Little beard? Auroraman threw his head back and nailed her in the nose. The back of his head lit up with pain as it smacked the icy hard surface of her face. He ignored the pain, used it, and fired his elbows behind him, striking her in the ribcage, anything to get some distance between him and her.

A large chunk of the ceiling came down, and Auroraman had to sharply fly him and Eve to the side to dodge it. He wanted to tell Axiom-man to watch what he was doing, but with Eve's arm pressing against his throat, he couldn't muster the words let alone breathe.

He got close to the roof and saw Axiom-man wrestling with Adam.

FROZEN STORM

Axiom-man punched Adam square in the face then shook out his hand from the pain of the impact. *A little too hard there.*

Axiom-man glanced below and saw Crystallion was buried beneath the rubble.

The roof was almost clear. Despite Adam grabbing at him from the front, he flew up and punched out the remainder of the roof, sending large, icy chunks down to the heap below.

Auroraman flew past him, dragging Eve with him on his back. He also dragged a green bubble filled with ice creatures with him and through the roof.

He disappeared through the opening.

Axiom-man turned his attention to Adam and gave him a double punch to the stomach before kicking him mid-air and sending him to the large debris of ice below.

Auroraman dumped off the ice creatures inside the courtyard then focused his attention solely on Eve. She growled and hissed at him. He punched her in the face then in the neck, then created a giant hammer construct with his staff and smacked her away. She tumbled to the ground below, then quickly turned upward to face him and create an ice path heading back toward him. Auroraman built a giant shield out of his staff's energy just in time to block one of her punches. The second came through, and her icy fist sent his head so far to the left he felt a vertebrae slip out of place. It cracked back in when he jolted his head to center.

A.P. FUCHS

He needed to beat her, but there was someone under there, someone innocent. He needed her unconscious and didn't know how else to do it other than brute force. He hammered away on her, driving his boxing-gloved-constructed fists into her head over and over.

Finally, it seemed she began to weaken. He kept going, never letting up. It was like fighting steel. Only time and consistent force had a chance to break it. Not that he wanted her to smash into a million pieces, but he had to knock her out.

Had to.

Auroraman kept fighting.

Eve made one final effort with a kick to Auroraman's gut. The blow almost made him hurl. He used a net made of a chains construct and shot Eve to the ground. The green chains pinned her and held her to the ground.

"Good enough for now," Auroraman said and flew back to where Axiom-man was.

Axiom-man punched at Adam but got nowhere.

The rubble below began to stir. Any second now Crystallion would emerge.

"Need a hand?" Auroraman said and shot another chain net out from his staff. It wrapped around Adam, dropping him to the ground. Axiom-man didn't know the staff could work at a distance, that is, keep constructs alive even though they weren't touching the staff.

"Nice trick," Axiom-man said.

"It's a new one I've learned," Auroraman said with a smile.

The rubble stirred some more, and Crystallion burst forth.

FROZEN STORM

Without hesitating, both heroes flew toward him, each taking a side and driving Crystallion up against the wall.

"Turn these people back now!" Axiom-man said.

Crystallion merely grinned and shot two ice beams from his fists, blowing the heroes away.

Axiom-man tumbled back through the air and managed to right himself after a few spins. Auroraman landed on his belly and slid backward across the ice. The two went for Crystallion again. This time, Axiom-man landed a punch to his jaw then was grabbed by the neck and tossed to the side. He slammed up against the wall, soon covered in ice from a blast from Crystallion's hand. Auroraman took a swipe at him with his staff, only to meet the same fate.

"Fools," Crystallion said. "Why fight something you cannot stand against?"

Because that's what we do, Axiom-man thought. He powered up his eye beams and used them to carve himself out of the ice. Auroraman did something similar with his staff, then used the green glowing globe to create a protective aura around himself.

The two flew at Crystallion. Axiom-man fired from his eye beams, hitting Crystallion in the shoulders, making him stumble back a step. He then flew behind him and shot behind his knees, making Crystallion buckle. Auroraman created a giant hammer construct and swung it down on Crystallion as if measuring sledgehammer strength at a fair.

Crystallion went down into the ice, then quickly shot himself up, riding poles of ice on either side of him.

Axiom-man flew again, eyes charged, and this time put more power behind it. He struck Crystallion in the face, the chest, front of the knees, even his ankles.

Crystallion fell and went down on one knee then shot a blast of ice at Axiom-man. Before Axiom-man could react, Auroraman stood in front of him, stopping the attack with a giant green shield.

"Thanks," Axiom-man said.

"Don't mention it," Auroraman replied. "We need to come up with something new. This guy's unbeatable."

Chapter Nineteen

"What else is there?" Axiom-man asked.

"I don't know. That's the prob—" Auroraman clamped his mouth shut and focused on thickening the shield. Ice ray after ice ray beat against it until one large one shattered the shield.

With a battle cry, Axiom-man flew toward Crystallion at what Auroraman assumed was his top speed. Just as it looked like Axiom-man was going to hit Crystallion head first and knock himself out, he changed course and veered slightly to the side and let Crystallion have it in the stomach with a right hook. Axiom-man then spun around behind their foe and came back from the other side, doing the same to Crystallion's lower back.

Auroraman noticed Crystallion's eyes began to glow—then out shot ice rays straight at him. Auroraman put up another shield then, concentrating, created a green cannon that poked itself through the middle of the shield. He fired the thing; Crystallion took the blow, but seemed to finally start to weaken.

"Keep at him!" Auroraman said.

"On it!" Axiom-man replied.

With a roar, Crystallion stretched a hand out to either side then spun like a tornado, shooting ice and snow until there wasn't a place to hide. Axiom-man veered to the side and got under a green bubble from Auroraman's staff.

"Okay, he's not weakening," Auroraman said.

"No," Axiom-man said, "and things are about to get worse." He looked upward to where Adam and Eve stood atop the opening in the roof.

Auroraman swallowed the dry lump in his throat; he heard Axiom-man inhale a deep breath through his nose and blow it out his mouth.

Adam and Eve slid down a pair of ice slides and landed beside their master.

Crystallion pointed at Auroraman and Axiom-man. "Destroy them."

Adam and Eve took off to the left and right, then did a sharp turn inward at the same time. It was if they were linked somehow. Their movements . . . such unison.

Adam took a swipe at Axiom-man. He dodged it and delivered a hard punch to Adam's icy gut then, using the same hand, came up in an uppercut and knocked Adam's head back. In an instant, icy arms were around his waist, squeezing the life out of him. Axiom-man rained down blows on Adam's shoulders, pile-driving him as hard as he could to get the menace to let go. When he finally did, Axiom-man was so winded he dropped to one knee and needed a second to catch his breath. Adam's ice fists slammed down on Axiom-man's back, sending him sprawling onto the ground. He quickly flipped over and fired his energy beams at Adam's chest and abdomen, pushing Adam back. Axiom-man floated up and righted himself, then flew straight at Adam, hooking him about the waist and flying him straight into the ice wall beyond. Adam hit the wall with a sickening smack despite him being made of ice himself. As fast as he could, Axiom-man punched Adam in the face over and over, trying to knock him out. He doubted it was even possible, but he had to try.

FROZEN STORM

Adam grabbed Axiom-man by the side of the arms and threw him across the room. Axiom-man bumped into Crystallion as he flew past and the behemoth of an ice man grabbed him and tossed him back to Adam as if he weighed nothing. Adam took Axiom-man and drove him into the floor. As strong as Axiom-man's aura was, it could only take so much, and his body hurt and ached all over. He could only imagine the bruises and swelling. He heard Auroraman and Eve fighting elsewhere in the room: sounds of punches being thrown and blasts from Auroraman's staff.

All Axiom-man knew at that moment was this had to end.

Now.

Auroraman had Eve locked between his body and his staff. She tried firing ice rays from her eyes at him, but he dodged side to side, not giving her a solid focal point. He eyed his staff then, as if the staff obeyed the direction of his gaze, he moved his eyes to Eve, a green flow of energy following his sightline. It drilled into the side of Eve's head and soon she screamed and went limp. Auroraman dropped her, stepped over her, then faced her from behind. She rolled over and slowly got to her feet. Not wanting to fight anymore, Auroraman created another green bubble, hoping to encase her and once more get her out of the throne room. As the bubble began to close in around her, she reached out and shot ice rays from her hands, stopping the bubble from fully forming. Auroraman concentrated even more, but her ice rays overpowered him and the bubble disintegrated.

Damn, he thought. *Dammit!* He shot another ray of energy at her, sending her sprawling against the wall.

Elsewhere in the room, Axiom-man and Adam exchanged blows.

Auroraman lunged at Eve and put away all sense of decency and propriety. This wasn't about a man fighting a woman. This was about a man fighting evil, and he had to use all force necessary to take her down.

She shot ice rays at him again and Auroraman blocked them with a glowing shield. He then fired the shield at her, its solid form crushing her further against the wall. When the shield dissipated, Eve stood against the wall, groaning.

Adam was suddenly thrown up against the wall beside her, Axiom-man pinning him against the wall with his eye beams.

"We can't do this forever," Axiom-man shouted over Adam's growls.

"I know. I'm getting tired," Auroraman replied.

"Tired?"

"You know what I mean." Auroraman steered his green ray toward Axiom-man's eye beams, hoping the impact of the combined energy would stop Adam but not kill him.

Adam screamed the moment the two beams combined. His body started to convulse.

From behind, Crystallion shouted something, but Auroraman couldn't make it out.

Eve dove at Auroraman, trying to get him to stop attacking Adam. Auroraman kicked her away, then nodded at Axiom-man and the two focused their energy beams at her.

She screamed and shook, the energy too much. They focused the beams on her until she stopped moving, then

FROZEN STORM

they focused the beams back at Adam. He lay there on the ground, kept down by the beams' combined power. Eve crawled over to him and lay on top of him as if to shield him. Auroraman and Axiom-man did not relent and let her have it. As long as she wouldn't die, Auroraman decided to give her everything he had.

A whoosh on the air jolted Auroraman's attention away from what he was doing and Crystallion got in front of Adam and Eve and absorbed most of the energetic blows the two men threw off.

"Now you fall," Crystallion said.

Crystallion shot ice beams from his hands; the heroes dove and dodged to either side. He shot at them again, this time striking them both. A sudden shock of cold raced through Axiom-man's system even with the aura. He couldn't believe how cold this guy was or how it was even possible to generate such ice. Crystallion was upon him and drove a fist straight into Axiom-man's face, breaking his nose. Blood ran down his mouth beneath his mask and quickly began to crust over thanks to the cold in the room.

Auroraman stood strong with his staff and seemed to send as much energy as possible in Crystallion's direction. The green beam hit him and slowly pushed him away from Axiom-man. Once he obtained enough distance, Auroraman went up to Axiom-man and asked, "Are you all right?"

Axiom-man brushed at his nose with his sleeve even though it didn't help—the blood had frozen already—and said, "I'll live."

"But for how long?"

"Which is why this has to stop. Those two others are down for the count right now, but this ain't over. We need to do this together."

Auroraman nodded and just as he planted his feet, Crystallion rushed him like a raging bull. When he slammed into him, Auroraman went sailing through the air. Axiom-man flew at Crystallion, pummeling his fists into him anywhere he could find an opening. He hoped that the combined power of his flight speed and ultra strength would send the guy to his knees.

Out of his peripheral, Axiom-man caught Auroraman retrying to get into position: feet planted firm, both hands on the staff, jaw clenched.

"Fire!" Axiom-man shouted.

Auroraman did.

Axiom-man gave Crystallion a final strike then joined his comrade and shot his eye beams at him.

Crystallion fell to his knees, and for a second, Axiom-man thought they had him.

"Keep firing!" Axiom-man said.

"Roger that!" Auroraman replied.

Slowly, Crystallion got to his feet and began a slow walk toward them, pushing against their combined power. Snow and ice crystals began to form around his fists. His hands slowly raised and any second—

"No!" Axiom-man shouted and readjusted his eye beams so they went *through* Auroraman's globe, mixing with the mysterious, green-glowing energy.

Crystallion shrieked and he began to shake. His head knocked back and he opened his mouth. Black smoke began to leak out and Axiom-man recognized it as the black cloud of the portal.

Auroraman must have seen it, too, because he said, "The cloud! My globe's going nuts. It's your ride home."

FROZEN STORM

"I can't leave you."

"We've got this. We're hurting him. Keep firing, but the second you see any opening to go home, you have to take it."

Energy still pouring from his eyes, Axiom-man said, "If I go and he recovers, you will die."

Grimacing, Auroraman said, "Then I die."

The black cloud pooled out of Crystallion's mouth, enshrouding him in darkness.

The two men kept on the heat and soon Crystallion's cries ceased. The two powered down, but the moment he emerged from the cloud, they let him have it again.

Adam and Eve stirred off to the side.

A black cloud once again covered Crystallion.

Not sure what he was going to do when he reached him, Axiom-man flew toward Crystallion, grabbed hold of his icy body, and drove him into the cloud, only to emerge in darkness.

Chapter Twenty

Auroraman powered down, then turned to face Adam and Eve. He took one quick glance back at the black cloud, and it drew in on itself, sealing itself shut and was no more.

Auroraman tapped his staff against his palm like a batter approaching home plate. "All right. Who's next?"

In the darkness, Crystallion punched and kicked Axiom-man, clearly trying to take him down. But the blows—they were so much softer here, yet Axiom-man couldn't linger too long. The cloud was his weakness, and soon its surrounding pressure made him fold over. Nausea gripped him, and he wrapped his hands around his stomach.

Crystallion took a swing at him. Axiom-man blocked it and punched him back.

Light.

The ambient glow of light came from behind. Axiom-man looked over his shoulder and saw a snowy street. He hoped it wasn't a street from Humboldt, but rather one from Winnipeg. He flew toward it. Crystallion grabbed him by his heels, spun him around, and threw him into the dark. Using the glow from his eye beams to enable him to see, Axiom-man flew right back at him and pinned him to the ground. He rained down blow after blow, both to stop him and to work out the hard choice he was going to have to make: Crystallion couldn't come back with him. If exposed to the ice and snow again, it

FROZEN STORM

might return him to full strength, and what happened in Humboldt would happen in Winnipeg. Axiom-man couldn't have that.

"I'm sorry," he said and delivered the hardest hit he could muster, knocking Crystallion out.

Axiom-man then flew toward the slit in the darkness, picking up speed as the thing began to shrink. He managed to squeak through it and tumbled onto the icy streets of what he immediately recognized as home.

Eyes still powered up, he lay there in the snow, his gaze never leaving what was left of the black cloud. What felt like ten long minutes went by even though it was probably only a few seconds, and the cloud vanished.

It was over.

Adam and Eve got to their feet. They staggered a few steps then came at Auroraman. He shot at them with his staff, driving them back, their strength and fortitude seeming much less than they had been before.

He got in between them and used the staff as a club against each of their heads and put them down.

Auroraman gazed around the room. The snow that seemed to consistently fall when Crystallion was around stopped and settled on the ground. Auroraman flew up and over the wall, only to see hordes of ice creatures below. Except for maybe a scant few, this could very well be the entire town of Humboldt. The thing was, the creatures didn't try and jump up and attack him. They only mingled around like a bunch of zombies, seeming to not know whether they were coming or going.

Except for—hopefully—these people returning to normal, it was over.

And Auroraman didn't even have a chance to say goodbye to his new ally.

Perhaps one day their paths would cross again.

Perhaps not.

All he knew was they had needed to do this together. There had been no other way.

Auroraman took off into the air to survey the rest of the town.

He hoped to God nothing else would go wrong.

Epilogue

ONE WEEK LATER...

THE TOWN OF Humboldt had finally begun to thaw out; the snow and ice left behind by Crystallion and Adam and Eve was so cold it took a week to melt, even with plus-twenty temperatures. With Crystallion gone, the townspeople had returned to normal, even Adam and Eve. Auroraman wished he knew their real names and wanted to explain to them what happened. He hadn't gotten a chance to and was instead preoccupied with cleaning up the town.

He learned that despite the people turning back to normal, they retained the memory of what happened. Perhaps, in a way, Crystallion won after all. Now, these poor people were stuck with the memory of the horrors they became and what they had done. He wished Axiom-man was around so they could talk it over, but his heart ached at the idea of never seeing his new ally again. Then again, if he could shoot green energy from a staff and Axiom-man could fly and ice creatures could manifest, it was impossible to tell what the future might bring.

He just hoped that one day, even if just for a moment, he'd see his friend again.

The sound of sirens rose on the air.

Auroraman rose into the air, too.

He had a job to do.

"Get away from me, man, get away from me!" the thief screamed, running down a back alley.

Axiom-man dropped down in front of him. "Get away from you? Don't think so." He grabbed the thief by the arm and yanked the purse the guy had ripped off some poor old lady from his hands. "Now let's return this then you and I are heading to some other boys in blue."

The thief punched at him. Axiom-man head butted him hard enough to daze him, then dragged him along.

Another fresh crime wave was sweeping the city and bodies were showing up everywhere.

Redsaw was at work.

It was time for Axiom-man to go to work, too.

AFTERWORD

by
Jeff Burton

So, by the time you read this I am hoping you have fully enjoyed reading the team up of Axiom-man and my character, Auroraman. Two Canadian prairie-based superheroes from two very different worlds. If you haven't had the chance to read anything Auroraman yet, I would suggest picking up *The Adventures of Auroraman* No. 1. Housed within its massive 64 pages are eight different adventures, including the six-page prelude to this novel.

I love a good superhero team up story, always have. The chance to see characters that aren't normally together share the page and stage is something that, in my mind, can be extremely rewarding and fun. That's why when I was first approached by A.P. Fuchs about teaming up our characters I didn't need to think too hard or long about if I wanted to or not. Truth be told, I had already talked with him a couple of times about team up ideas for comic stories, but this time it was different: it was in his medium of the superhero novel. It has been a grand adventure—sharing ideas, batting back and forth how the characters would meet, where the story would take place, the villain(s), and on and on. It was also important we ensured both characters would have the chance to shine. I became a big fan of the Axiom-man character and stories after meeting A.P. Fuchs a few years ago so to have him ask to write a story featuring Auroraman was a pretty big deal to me.

At the time of this writing, I have had the chance to read through the first draft of the novel, something I've been told has never happened before in A.P. Fuchs's career. I feel very honoured to have had the chance to see it in an unpolished state. Even before the edits and fine tuning I could see it was an amazingly well-crafted tale and one I cannot wait to have on my bookshelf.

Thank you for coming along on this ride and I hope you have enjoyed it as much as I have.

- Jeff Burton
Humboldt, SK

About the Authors

A.P. Fuchs is the author of many novels and short stories. His most recent efforts of putting pen to paper are *Flash Attack: Thrilling Stories of Terror, Adventure, and Intrigue; The Canister X Transmission: Year Three; Axiom-man Episode No. 3: Rumblings;* and *Mech Apocalypse.*

Also a cartoonist, he is known for his superhero series, *The Axiom-man Saga*, both in novel and comic book format.

Fuchs's main website is **www.canisterx.com**

> Join his free weekly newsletter at
> **www.tinyletter.com/apfuchs**

The Adventures of Auroraman creator and writer **Jeff Burton** is a father of five and a teacher from Humboldt, Saskatchewan. Given the inspiration for Auroraman from a dear friend, Ted Green, Jeff mentored under Andrew Lorenz (S17 Productions) and together they fleshed out the concept and co-scripted the #0 issue of *Auroraman*.

Jeff takes his lead from the fond memories of reading fun comic books as a child and loves to see that reaction in his own kids and his students when he introduces them to comics, be it Auroraman or many of the other great Canadian independent comic books.

GET THE SAGA AND HIT THE SKIES

Available in paperback and eBook at your favorite on-line retailer or through your local bookstore.

www.canisterx.com

Find the Prelude to Frozen Storm in
issue #1 of The Adventures of Auroraman!

Follow Auroraman on Facebook to keep up on all
the news and to order the latest issues!